THE
TAPESTRY
OF
SPIRIT

ERIK PAUL ROCKLIN

ELUCIDARÉ

PRESS

Publisher's Cataloging-in-Publication data is as follows:
Rocklin, Erik Paul.
The tapestry of spirit / Erik Paul Rocklin.
p. cm.
ISBN 978-0-615-59569-6
1. Spirituality --Fiction. 2. Spiritual life --Fiction. 3. Journeys --Fiction.
4. New age fiction. I. Title.
PS3618.O354468 Ta 2012
813.6 --dc23   2012935478

Printed in the United States of America

ISBN-13: 978-0-615-59569-6
ISBN-10: 0-615-59569-3

For Ma.

❧ 1 ❧

That night, the boy had a vivid dream, unlike any other in its clarity and crispness. But as clear as the images were in the dream, their meaning was not.

The dream began with the boy in the darkness just before the dawn, kneeling and facing East as the glow of the approaching Sun neared the horizon. Although cold throughout his body, the boy waited, patiently, as the Eastern sky continued to brighten.

A moment more and the first light of the Sun had appeared, its touch to the boy's skin immediately warming and comforting him. As he knelt, with more and more of the light and warmth from the rising Sun bathing him, he closed his eyes, and when he opened them again, he found himself standing alone in the center of the city in the large, circular marketplace that he had been to many, many times before.

Normally a bustling gathering of merchants, travelers, and residents of the city, all busy around tents, tables, and stalls, the marketplace was now completely empty and silent, a state of which the boy had never seen. The Sun was directly overhead, and because of that, it cast no shadows.

There, standing in the center of the circular marketplace, the lone boy turned in a slow circle, surveying its edges as if scanning the degrees of a compass. With the Sun in a position directly overhead and casting no shadows, the boy did not know his direction, but he felt compelled in the dream to determine, for some reason, which direction was East, the direction in which he had knelt at the beginning of his dream.

The boy relied purely on his feelings to ascertain this, and when contentment, purity, and a sense of a return to the familiar were all strong within him, he believed himself to have found East. And in doing so, the boy again closed his eyes.

When he opened his eyes next, the boy was in a warm, dim place, somehow beneath the soil of the World, surrounded by walls that gently moved before his eyes. Again the boy attempted to discern which direction was East, but being below the soil of the World and again without the Sun above for reference, the boy could only slowly turn in place until he again had the feeling of the familiar, and when it was strong within him, believed again that he had found the East.

Directly in front of him was a portion of the moving wall, which, before his eyes, began to appear more and more solid, and as it solidified, a figure began to take shape within it. Blurry at first, it gradually began to resemble something…a young man…a young man in Mage's garb.

The boy awoke abruptly.

Although the whole of the dream was unlike any other that the boy had had, the appearance of the Mage was familiar to him, for as a boy, he had frequent dreams of the Mage; a figure that, to him, was always comforting while in his presence, and always left the boy with a sense of clarity, of possibility, and of hope upon his wakening.

This had always confused the boy, as generally, Mysticism and those who practiced it were scorned, and branded as blasphemous heretics, so that to even mention them, even in the context of a dream, was to bring to one great scrutiny, social discrimination, and even fear of death. But to the boy, the memories of the Mage in his dreams were always pure, and of hope for what could be.

For in his dreams of the Mage, the boy always had an unspoken sense that they understood each other, that there was a familiarity with the Mage that was uncommon to anything else, either in his dreams or while awake.

The boy's Mother, whom he would always tell of his dreams of the Mage, was always encouraging of them, and had great interest in the details within them. Yet she also made a secret pact with the boy, one in which neither of them would ever discuss his dreams of the Mage with others, for fear of what may befall the boy.

So it was the dream of the Mage the night prior that had returned several things to the boy when he woke; feelings of hope and serenity brought by the return of the Mage, and feelings of hope and serenity brought by the memories of his Mother.

And in reflection on his childhood spent with her, hopeful words, spoken by her several seasons before her passing, returned to the boy's thoughts, in which she told the boy that one day, he would realize the beautiful gifts that he could offer the World.

And with the return of these thoughts to his mind came other words to his ears, words that she had uttered with great pride on one occasion when she recognized that very soon, his path would lead him away, although not of his decision.

'To the World I give my son, and to my son I give the World,' she had said.

They were words that the boy understood, although he felt that they had additional meaning within them that he had yet to realize.

But it was after her unexpected passing that the boy—nearly a man in stature, yet not one by age—was forced to live as a man in the World of men, and from that season since, the dreams of the Mage became less and less frequent, finally to test the boy's memory as to when he had dreamt of him last.

For the boy, he now was living in the World of men, and there could be no changing of the past.

And so, the boy spent that day as any other, with parts of the dream of the Mage returning to his thoughts on several occasions: the oddity of the empty circle of the marketplace, the pull from the East, and the appearance of the Mage in the moving walls beneath the soil of the World.

That night, the boy had the identical dream again, and upon awakening the following morning, he decided that the second occurrence of the same dream was something to be heeded, and that he would go to the marketplace that day.

And so, at mid-day, with the Sun in a position to cast no shadows, the boy went to the center of the marketplace. But unlike in his dream, it was now its usual bustling gathering of people engaged in the bartering of buying and selling.

The boy made his way to the center of the marketplace and stood, unsure of what he was to expect. He stood for an uneventful moment, and then decided to scan the edges of the marketplace as he had done in his dream, although he knew not what he might be looking for.

As he slowly surveyed the edges of the marketplace through the flow of people passing by, he caught a glimpse of a dark figure near the edge of one of the rows of merchant stalls. The figure was unmoving, facing the boy, and wore a dark robe, including a dark hood that completely hid the face within it.

Although the boy could not make out the features of the figure, he could feel a presence. It was a presence that was at once both familiar and cold, and for some reason, the boy felt compelled to leave the marketplace, yet he stood where he was, determined to understand if his dream was to lead to something.

As the boy studied the dark figure across the crowded distance, the boy was perplexed. There was no dark figure in his dream, so questions emerged within the boy. Was the figure important? Was it a part of his Destiny? Did the figure offer answers to the unspoken questions within the boy?

Given that the figure seemed to be mirroring him across the marketplace, the boy concluded that it must be meaningful, so he began to make his way toward it. But after a few steps through the flowing crowd, the boy looked up to find that the dark figure was gone. He stopped and scanned the nearby area, but the figure was now nowhere to be seen.

Confused, the boy decided to return to the center of the marketplace and scan its edges yet again, and as he did, he noticed another figure on the opposite edge of the great, crowded circle.

This figure was also motionless, as the dark figure had been, but clothed in average garb, and without a hood to conceal his features. Through the moving crowd of people, the boy could see that it was an old man not much taller than he, with grey hair and beard, and tanned skin. The old man was facing the boy, and when the boy's eyes made contact with his, the old man smiled. At this, the boy felt a different presence than that of the dark figure, this time experiencing a feeling that was at once both familiar and warm.

The boy then began his way toward the old man, looking up frequently to find that he still waited for him at the edge of the marketplace, and as the boy finally emerged from the flow of people, he stood in front of the old man, who was still smiling.

And as they stood, eye-to-eye since the boy was tall for his young age, the boy also wondered if this man was a hidden part of his dream. The same questions emerged within the boy as had when he considered the dark figure. Was the old man important? Was he a part of the boy's Destiny? Did he offer answers to the unspoken questions within the boy?

As curious and intrigued as the boy found himself to be about the old man, he struggled to find the words for even a basic greeting. After all, the old man may just be a friendly stranger, having nothing to do with the boy or his dreams or the unspoken questions within him. He may be a traveler passing through. He may be someone local to the area who had seen the boy before.

As the words to begin a conversation continued to elude the boy, and doubt that his actions were now simply of pure silliness, it was the old man who spoke, saying simply:

"I can help you to understand your dream," to which the boy continued to have no words.

The Elder and the boy sat at a small table in a nearby merchant's tent and drank tea as they spoke of the boy's dream.

"Dreams are mystical," said the old man, "for they show us what we see but are often unable to recognize. Always regard and respect your dreams, for they come from the source of truth. They come from the Tapestry of Spirit."

"The Tapestry of Spirit?" asked the boy, having never heard of such a thing.

"We are all a part of it from the moment of our birth," explained the Elder, "a fact which will never change. But while we are all a part of it, our place within it is different for each of us, as we all journey different paths. But despite the differences of clans and tribes across the lands of the World, we all share it, and we all share its essence. The Tapestry of

Spirit will never betray us, although we can betray it by denying our natural relationship to it."

"I have heard no one ever speak of it," said the boy.

"Among those who live in the darkness, it is denied, ignored, and unrecognized," replied the Elder. "Among those who live within its light, it is as obvious as the Sun that rises in the East with every day. I am one of many that assist in the journey from the darkness to the light."

The Elder took a sip of his spiced tea before continuing, eyeing the silent but attentive boy.

"To have awareness of it arise within you is a profound event, the first step of many, if you are willing to walk them."

The words of the Elder resonated within the boy, and although he was not certain of it, a feeling within him stirred that made him believe that the Elder sitting before him indeed represented a path to the answers of his unspoken questions.

"Will it help me to find my Destiny?" asked the boy.

The Elder smiled at the depth of the question from the boy of so few seasons, but was not surprised by it.

"Your Destiny Thread does not need to be found, it only needs to be remembered," answered the Elder. "Just as each of us is a part of the Tapestry of Spirit, each of us has a Thread of Destiny from it, and like the Tapestry of Spirit, your Destiny Thread exists within you and has from your birth, and if lived, will lead you back to the Tapestry of Spirit. By seeking your Destiny Thread, you seek the Tapestry of Spirit, although this may not be clear to you."

The boy stared at the Elder, contemplating the seemingly magical details of his explanation, and became skeptical despite the things of which he spoke that stirred intrigue in the boy. It was an unfortunate habit that he had acquired since living as a boy in the World of men over the previous few seasons; to become cynical of things that sounded hopeful.

"And how can I be sure that you indeed are a true guide for a journey such as the one that you describe?" asked the boy. "Not merely another charlatan on the edges of the marketplace, speaking of things such as Destiny and Spirit, seeking the young and unsuspecting to swindle and lead astray, presuming to impress them with supposed knowledge of a dream that they may have had?"

The Elder calmly sipped his tea and then smiled.

"Because I know that your dream began at dawn, kneeling to the East, the direction in which all who seek their Destiny Thread will travel," said the Elder.

The truth of the Elder's insights instantly banished the boy's suspicions, and he sat, stunned at the knowledge that the old man sitting before him possessed of his dream.

"I did not seek you," continued the Elder, "it was you who summoned me."

The boy continued to sit in astounded silence, and a feeling that he had not felt for several seasons began to rise within him; a feeling of hope. Hope in a belief that the Elder was indeed a key to his dream and his search for his Destiny. But despite this hope, and the Elder showing that he knew much of the boy's dream, the boy found himself afraid to ask if the Elder also knew of the Mage within his dream, for he knew not how the Elder might react, and because of that, chose not to mention it.

"You should understand that, once begun, the journey will hold perils," continued the Elder. "As much as you believe that you walk freely among the shadows of the World, that they are merely cast from the passing of the Sun in the sky along your journey, this is not always the truth. The shadows of the World, if allowed, will often direct and control your journey in ways that are not true to the Tapestry of Spirit. These shadows will become especially vigilant on your journey East, and will conspire in an effort to keep you in darkness and prevent you from completing it. You may have already sensed the darkness that exists within them."

The boy thought of the dark figure that he saw on the other side of the marketplace, and of what it made him feel.

"These dark forces will take many shapes, both familiar and unfamiliar to you," continued the Elder. "They will attempt to distance you from your Destiny Thread and therefore the

Tapestry of Spirit. They will attempt to cover them, to disguise them, to sway your mind to yield its belief in them, so it is during those moments that you must in fact rely on your belief in them most of all."

"These forces, they are obvious to you?" asked the boy.

"Yes," replied the Elder, "but just as taking the journey is your decision alone, so must your confronting of the shadows be. I can be of guidance to you along the journey, but I cannot face or defeat the dark shadows that you alone must eventually gain awareness and mastery of."

As the boy considered all of what he was hearing, the Elder took another sip of his tea before continuing.

"You should also understand that this journey, once started and if successful, shall conclude, and upon its conclusion you will exist in a World different than the one that you know of now. You may return to familiar people and places, but they may not be the same."

The Elder paused, looking deeply into the boy's eyes as he spoke a final, solemn statement.

"The journey consists of a course that, once traveled, cannot be returned to obscurity."

The boy felt the gravity of the Elder's words. He vaguely sensed of the dangers that he spoke of, and that things in his life would be forever changed if he commenced and completed the journey, although he did not know specifically how. Yet despite the hope and promise of what the journey could reveal, the boy felt an unusual fear and sadness that his life as he knew it would be different, as, although his life was filled with darkness and unspoken questions, its familiarity provided some comfort in the string of his blurred days.

The Elder sat patiently as the boy grappled with his feelings. After a moment and with things carefully considered, the boy finally spoke again and asked a simple question.

"When can this journey begin?"

❧ 3 ❧

The following morning, just before dawn, the boy arrived back at the marketplace as instructed by the Elder when they had parted the previous afternoon. The merchants were just arriving to display their wares, and at the center of the empty marketplace stood the Elder with two leather packs on the ground beside him.

As the boy approached, he remarked to the Elder on the packs lying on the ground.

"No horses?" asked the boy.

"This journey is meant to be taken by foot, one step at a time," replied the Elder, who then lifted one of the packs from the ground and handed it to the boy, who slung it onto his back. For such a grand journey as the Elder had described, the boy thought, the pack seemed small and felt light upon his back and shoulders. The Elder lifted the other pack to his own shoulder, and he and the boy began walking toward the East.

As they left the marketplace and walked down one of the city roads, the boy could not help but ask about the contents of the packs that they carried. He was curious as to if they would be sufficient for the journey.

"Will these supplies sustain us?" he asked.

"If we have needs along the way, they will be provided for," said the Elder. "It is the way of the journey."

As they continued, the boy studied the Elder's slim frame as he walked by his side, and although he was thin, he appeared quite fit, with a certain subtle strength and energy to him that gave the boy confidence in his stamina and guidance. Although the boy had not yet known the old man for a single, full day, he felt curiously protected in his presence.

As they approached the outskirts of the city, the boy was surprised to see a great, grey cloud quickly approaching from the East, and the boy smelled dampness in the air as a gentle breeze met them.

"Perhaps we should delay the start of the journey, for there is rain in that cloud," said the boy, stopping in his steps, startled at how quickly the cloud had approached overhead.

"Just as you have summoned me, you have also summoned the cloud," said the Elder. "Its rain will fall when your journey begins, whether it be today, tomorrow, or many days from now. But when its rain does fall, it will not fall for long."

The boy did not understand what the Elder had said about his summoning of the cloud, and was further intrigued at how it, once quickly approaching, had now reached a position directly over the edge of the city and had stopped there, suspended in the sky, advancing no further.

With a trust in the truth of the Elder's words, the boy nodded and they proceeded to leave the city, and just as the Elder had said, no sooner had they taken twenty steps when the cloud began to rain down upon them.

It was a heavy rain, but it was oddly gentle, and it was not long before it had soaked the boy to his skin. But unlike other rains that would have chilled the boy in that time of the season, this rain was warming, and provided a sense of comfort, and instead of his wet pack and clothes weighting down the boy, he felt curiously lighter. It was this sensation that brought memories back to the boy of when he was a child, and how, when it would rain, he and his Mother would go out into the heaviest of it and dance and laugh and reach their outstretched arms up to the sky to embrace the falling drops. And with the return of those memories, the boy felt cleansed, purified, and young again.

As the boy fondly reminisced, the rain suddenly subsided as quickly as it had begun, also just as the Elder had said it would, and to the boy's amazement, the cloud quickly retreated back toward the East from where it had come and disappeared beyond the horizon.

As they walked throughout the morning, the Elder noticed the boy regularly looking back behind them, and with each glance backward to the city that continued to move further and further from sight, the boy walked with less and less conviction in each step.

"Familiarity does not equate to truth, nor does it necessarily equate to your Thread of Destiny," said the Elder softly, sensitive to what the boy was feeling.

A few moments later, the boy glanced backward to find the city now completely out of sight, but as the Elder had hoped, intention soon returned to the boy's steps as they continued the journey to the East.

By mid-day, the Sun had dried their clothing and packs, and the boy and the Elder stopped to share a meal. As they ate, the boy felt compelled to share more of his dream that had moved him to go to the center of the marketplace the day before. He reasoned that since the Elder knew of the other parts of his dream, perhaps he knew of all of it, and the boy wanted to know if there was special meaning to the Mage.

"Since you know the beginning of my dream that brought our paths together, do you also know of the Mage?" asked the boy tentatively.

"Indeed," replied the Elder with a smile. "All guides, including myself, are of the Mage."

The boy was astonished and immediately felt great relief, and that the Elder himself was of the Mage inspired great curiosity within the boy.

"What is the Mage like?" asked the boy inquisitively.

"I have never met the Mage," said the Elder calmly, to which the boy's face contorted into confusion, not understanding how it could be that the Elder was of the Mage yet had never met the Mage.

"You dreamt of the Mage, not I," continued the Elder. "I only accompany and guide you along the journey to your meeting."

The boy was still confused.

"Is he my Destiny?" the boy asked, puzzled.

"The Mage waits at the conclusion of this journey, and it is only the Mage that can reveal how your Destiny Thread returns to the Tapestry of Spirit," replied the Elder. "Finding the Mage at that place enables vision beyond that of the eye."

"What vision is there beyond that of the eye?" asked the boy.

"Vision of the heart," replied the Elder, "and that is the most important vision to all people across the tribes and clans of the World, as it enables the connection of all things to the Tapestry of Spirit."

Although the boy did not understand all of the meaning within the words, he was nonetheless grateful for the additional insights of what his journey held. The boy's curiosity then turned to the Elder and what he had said about he and all other guides being of the Mage.

"So, there are more guides then?" asked the boy.

"Yes, many more," replied the Elder. "But guides only arrive when summoned, so their numbers will vary depending on the calls of the World. It is saddening that over the generations, our numbers have lessened."

The boy's thoughts returned to the journey, and to the Mage that the Elder said was waiting at its conclusion.

"I wonder what I will find at my Destiny," mused the boy aloud.

"One does not arrive at Destiny, one lives it," said the Elder. "It is not an answer but rather a thread of truth to live alongside as it winds like a river, revealing new things around every turn."

"But," started the confused boy, "my Destiny is what I am to be, is it not?"

The Elder smiled.

"You will meet another along your journey that will explain this to you," said the Elder.

The boy then understood that he would have to show patience for more of the answers to his questions.

❧ 4 ❧

Throughout the rest of the day's journey, the terrain began to roll gently and was sprinkled with more and more low desert shrub, and whereas they followed traveled roads out of the city when the journey began that morning, they now walked through untouched landscape, which concerned the boy.

"Should we not be on traveled roads?" he asked.

"The journeys East for those seeking their Destiny Thread are never the same," said the Elder, "for the starting point of each is always different. Existing paths do not determine your course, it is your new course that will determine your path."

By the setting of the Sun, they had found a low-lying area in the gently rolling landscape in which to spend the night. After eating, they sat beside a small fire in the darkness of the night, and as they talked of the day's travels, the boy was startled by the sound of footsteps approaching from the East.

Just as the boy and the Elder quickly reached their feet, the small fire illuminated a figure as it approached, revealing a young man dressed in dark, dirty, tattered garb. He labored in his steps and his breath was short, a weary, desperate look across his face.

"Greetings," gasped the man as he reached the boy and the Elder. "Apologies, I did not intend to alarm you."

The man stood before them, panting, his hands on his hips, as the boy and the Elder studied his weathered appearance.

"I am a traveler," the man said finally, looking to the boy.

"As are we," replied the boy, feeling a sudden sense of kinship with the man.

The man looked to the Elder and merely tipped his head, to which the Elder remained still.

"May I sit with you a while and rest?" asked the man, looking to the boy. "Fellow travelers should always harbor each other when in need."

"Of course," said the boy, for although he had never before left the city of his birth, he knew that it was indeed the way of those who traveled.

The three of them sat down around the small fire.

"My travels have fallen on misfortune," began the man sadly. "Ten moons ago, I began my travels to the East, in search of meaning, but roaming bandits ahead killed my guide and robbed me of everything, leaving me to die."

The boy was shocked and instantly became afraid. He looked to the Elder, who merely looked back calmly.

"Now, I travel back West, back home, to safety there," the man said, his weary gaze lost in the fire.

"But," he lamented, "I have nothing there now, having given all in order to travel East," he said softly. "That decision has cost me everything."

The boy's scared mind then began to fill with fear and doubt, and he wondered about his own decision to begin his journey, fearful that the same fate that had befallen the man also waited for he and the Elder.

The man looked up to the boy with sympathetic eyes. "I have not eaten in three days," he said. "Might I impose on you for some food and water?"

"Certainly," said the boy, quickly producing food and drink from his pack, the need to preserve it for his own journey suddenly a distant consideration. The hungry man eagerly accepted the food and began to eat.

The boy's worries returned to his own journey East, and that it would tragically end soon given the dangers that lay ahead, according to the man.

"Tell me more of these bandits," asked the boy nervously.

"They were as silent as the night," said the man through a mouthful of food, "appearing from the darkness before we knew of their presence."

The man paused, and when he spoke next, his voice trembled.

"They subjected my guide to the most gruesome of deaths, before my very eyes," he said, horror crossing his face and filling his eyes.

The boy looked to the Elder, who calmly looked back, as the man continued.

"They took all of our supplies and then left me to die, my hands and feet bound," he said. "But I was able to free myself, and since then, I have wandered West for the last three days until finding you here."

The man looked directly to the boy and said, "There is great danger ahead of you."

The boy looked again to the Elder, and meekly suggested to him, "Perhaps the course ahead should not be to the East?"

"The course is East," replied the Elder calmly yet firmly, his response doing nothing to ease the boy.

"But returning West will ensure your survival," said the frightened man, inserting himself into the exchange between the Elder and the boy. "And it may be that the bandits have learned of my escape and are now in pursuit," he added nervously, suddenly sitting upright and looking back into the darkness from where he had come.

The boy too peered nervously into the darkness from where the man had come.

"May I ask of you to stay at your camp tonight?" asked the man pleadingly of the boy.

"Of course," replied the boy, and then added, "and perhaps in the morning we will all return to the West together."

The man smiled at the boy in relief. "That pleases me to hear, as I do not wish to see your life end at such a young age."

"We will decide in the morning," stated the Elder firmly to them both. "I will remain awake through the night to watch for any danger that may approach," he said, which brought comfort to the boy.

The man finished eating the food he had been given, lay back on the ground, and was quickly asleep. The boy lay on the ground as well, and as he looked across the fire to the face of the Elder who remained sitting upright, he noticed that his gaze was upon the man.

Soon, the fatigue of the day's travel had drawn the boy into sleep.

The next morning, the boy awoke as the sky was just beginning to lighten from the glow of the Sun below the horizon. As he lay on the ground and cleared his eyes, the boy looked across from him to the Elder, who still sat upright from the night before, his eyes fixed on the man who remained sleeping on the ground beside the boy.

The night of sleep had done the boy good. With his body and mind rested, and the light of a new day filling the sky, he felt differently about the discussion from the night before. Whereas the blackness of the night brought fear and uncertainty, the brightening of the morning sky brought new determination to continue the journey, a journey that the boy hoped was to answer his unspoken questions.

The boy sat up and the Elder looked to him. The boy smiled, a confident smile, and the Elder knew that the boy had decided to continue his journey.

The sleeping man on the ground began to stir, and in a moment, sat upright.

"Forgive me my hosts," he said, abashed at being the last to wake, "but I have not slept much for the last three nights, and being here among you has allowed me much needed rest. I thank you for that."

The man looked about the camp for something that he could assist with.

"How can I help with our travels back to the West?" he asked.

"We will not be returning West," proclaimed the boy flatly, immediately drawing a concerned look from the man.

"I know these regions very well," added the Elder, "and how to avoid any bandits that may be lurking," to which the man eyed him with disbelief.

The man then looked back to the boy as the boy spoke.

"Do not fear for us, for my journey is one of great importance, and perils will exist along the way, this I understand."

The man took notice of the intention that the boy had laced his declaration with. He studied the boy for a moment longer, silence between them all.

"Very well then," said the man abruptly, adding politely, "may I ask you for another meal before I resume my travels alone to the West?"

The boy was inclined to again help a fellow traveler in need, and began to reach for his pack but was stopped short by a response from the Elder.

"We cannot spare another meal," said the Elder firmly. "The meal from last night will sustain you until you reach the city that lay only a day's travel ahead of you."

The man ignored the Elder's response, instead turning pleading eyes to the boy, but the boy remained motionless, heeding the Elder.

The man then abruptly stood up, seemingly void of all concern.

"I bid you safe travels," he said flatly, and left the camp, walking toward the West.

The boy and the Elder watched as he traversed the rolling terrain, and then disappeared beyond a low rise.

The boy contemplated the odd behavior of both the man and the Elder, and just as he was about to ask the Elder of it, the Elder spoke.

"Let us continue our journey without delay," said the Elder.

"But…" began the boy, his empty belly in need of food.

"We will eat after we are on our way," said the Elder calmly, to which they gathered themselves and their packs and resumed the journey East, toward the first light of the Sun that was just clearing the horizon.

It was only once the Sun had fully risen and had started its early path across the morning sky that they stopped and the Elder offered his explanation.

"That was not a fellow traveler," said the Elder, surprising the boy.

"It knew of our destination, as well as our origin, despite neither of us mentioning them. We traveled on no known road, yet it came to us across the darkness of the night. Its sole purpose was to convince you to abandon your journey to the East."

The Elder continued on to explain that the dark figures could arrive in any place, at any time, under any pretense, all to prevent the meeting of the Mage.

"Do you remember when we spoke in the marketplace of dark figures that would arise along your journey?" asked the Elder.

The boy recalled what the Elder had said, that figures of varying, recognizable as well as unrecognizable forms would arise, and would conspire to prevent his journey from concluding.

"I remember," replied the boy.

"That the forces would work to distance you from the Tapestry of Spirit?" continued the Elder.

"And that at those moments," recalled the boy aloud, "I was to rely on a belief in my Destiny Thread and the Tapestry of Spirit in order to sense their presence."

The Elder nodded.

The boy reflected on all that the Elder had said, and thought to himself that he would need to be more watchful for times when he felt that he was being pulled away from the light that would lead to the Tapestry of Spirit, and the answers to his unspoken questions. He thought of what the dark man had made him feel about his quest, a quest that earlier in the same day gave the boy hope and promise of things yet unrealized in his life.

"One who would instill fear in another in order to prevent one from following their Destiny Thread is not of the Tapestry of Spirit," said the Elder, "and such is the Nature of the dark figures. This attempt was to discourage you by creating something to fear that may lie ahead of you. There will be more attempts along your journey, and the closer you venture to the Tapestry of Spirit, the more sinister they will become."

The boy remembered the strength of the fear that he felt within himself at the words of the dark man.

"Could you not tell me of its presence last night?" asked the boy.

"You alone must cultivate your ability to sense the dark figures, for you alone must seek to understand their intention toward you. The decision to continue this journey is yours alone to make, as it must be. A journey made by force will not yield the meaning you seek. I can only offer my help and guidance along the way, if continuing is what you wish to do," said the Elder. "It is the way of our relationship, and there can be no changing it."

The boy nodded in understanding, then opened his pack to eat, now disappointed in its diminished contents from having given food to the dark man the prior night. He feared that the contents of his pack would not now sustain him, as he had suspected when he first saw the small pack on the ground next to the Elder back in the marketplace the day before.

Sensing the boy's concern, the Elder spoke.

"To give of yourself to dark figures only strengthens them, gives them hope, and at the same time, depletes you and threatens your journey," said the Elder.

The boy's concern returned to the contents of his pack.

"Have no worries," said the Elder, "for as I said, your needs will be met along the journey, as that too is the way."

Without understanding how, the boy was comforted by the words and the presence of the Elder, and they shared a meal in the warmth of the morning Sun before continuing East.

❧ 5 ❧

As they traveled the rest of that day, the terrain gradually changed to greener land with scattered shrubs and low trees.

That night, the boy had another dream. In it, he stood in near total darkness, with the only light coming from a large, simple, wooden frame that floated in the air in front of him. It was the type of frame that would hold a magnificent painting, the boy thought in the dream. But instead of the frame containing a painting, it held fog within its edges, a gently moving fog that was illuminated from within the frame somehow.

The boy cautiously wiped his hand through a part of the fog within the frame, and it cleared with a clean, distinct edge, not like a mist, and revealed a pair of eyes beyond. It startled the boy at first, but as he looked into the eyes beyond the fog, he became captivated by them. They were eyes of his own color, and in gazing into them the boy felt an odd feeling, as if in losing himself in them, he was found in them.

The boy blinked his eyes and was surprised that the eyes beyond the fog blinked as well. The boy continued to wipe away the fog cautiously, each pass revealing more and more of the illuminated contents within the frame.

After a moment, and with all fog wiped away, he was face to face with a young girl contained within the frame. She was about his age and almost an adult by stature, just as the boy was. She was dressed simply as he was, and although they were different beings, the boy felt a sense of oneness with the girl in the frame.

The boy smiled, to which the young girl smiled back.

The boy awoke, finding the Elder beside him just beginning to stir and wake in the dawn light, so the boy lay in silence for a few moments more, enjoying his dream of the meeting of the girl with his eyes.

After the Elder and the boy had both risen and eaten, they continued their journey East. The boy told the Elder of his dream of the girl. He described the darkness surrounding him, and the light from within the floating frame, and how, upon his clearing of the fog within the frame, the girl within was revealed.

"When looking into her eyes," said the boy, "I saw my own, as if a reflection."

"Muses come in many forms, and will often arrive in dreams," said the Elder.

"But, I am not a poet, an artist, or a philosopher," replied the boy, "and Muses come only to those capable of great achievements."

"We are all poets, artists, and philosophers," said the Elder flatly, "and even Muses ourselves."

The boy laughed aloud, not in impolite contestation of the Elder's statement, but in simple disbelief.

The Elder smiled at the boy, then asked a question of him to prove the truth in what he had said.

"Then tell me," asked the Elder, "how did you feel while in this dream?"

The boy spent a moment in contemplation before uttering the short, simple answer.

"Worthy."

The Elder smiled. "Worthy that your actions and your words can offer rhyme and artistry and wisdom to the World?"

The boy again assessed his feelings, then nodded affirmatively and smiled, and in that instant, he felt as if a man.

His thoughts returned to his Mother's words spoken only a few seasons prior, that one day, she said, he would realize the beautiful gifts that he could offer the World. It was the Muse in his dream that made the boy now believe that this was possible.

Throughout the morning, the boy reflected upon the events of the journey so far, and while there was much of it that was new and eventful and intriguing to him, doubts about these things somehow again found their way into his thoughts. After all, in the boy's young life, it seemed as if new and unexpected events always brought despair and hardship, and he wondered if the events of the past several days, as well as those that lie ahead, would eventually lead him to regret his decision to journey as he did.

While thoughts of seeking his Destiny Thread, the meeting of the Mage, and the Tapestry of Spirit kindled something within the boy that he hoped would lead to the answers to the unspoken questions within him, he could nonetheless not ignore the pull within him to return to the comfort of the dimmed, yet familiar path that his life followed prior to the start of the journey. He decided to share his thoughts with the Elder on this.

"Why do events of change bring despair?" asked the boy, the arbitrary nature of the question causing the Elder to pause in curiosity before replying.

"Because you are looking at them with vision of the eye and not of the heart," replied the Elder, "for change is in fact the greatest teacher along one's Destiny Thread, and should be valued as such."

The boy reflected on the words as the Elder continued.

"A thousand days spent the same will blur together, the end of one indistinguishable from the beginning of the next, all the while teaching one nothing but tolerance of monotony. But a thousand days spent differently will each be clear, with the change from one to the next giving color to the seasons, and lessons to the heart and mind. To progress along one's Destiny Thread is to live in change, for that is the way of life; change, and the lessons offered by it."

❧ 6 ❧

By mid-day, the boy and the Elder had come to the outskirts of a small city, and as they entered, the boy realized sadly that there was more doubt within him about continuing the journey than hope over what it offered. Despite the explanation by the Elder of change and its value along one's Destiny Thread, the young boy found himself with a silent desire to return to the city of his birth and continue living his simple life as it was. Perhaps his unanswered questions would be answered in another way, the boy wondered, perhaps it would just take time.

Once inside the small city, they found themselves on a crowded, narrow road, along whose length people traveled by foot and horse, and mules pulled carts and wagons. Merchant tents and stalls lined both sides of the road, and for the size of the small city, the boy was surprised at the number of people within it, and it seemed to him that the road itself could surely not hold another person or horse or mule.

As he and the Elder made their way down the crowded road, suddenly and from behind them they heard a scream, followed by more screams and shouts. The crowd they waded in suddenly heaved, and the entire mass of people in the road surged forward from the mysterious fear and panic that rose up behind them.

In the next instant, the crowd had become a desperate mob, with people pushing, running, falling, all of them desperate to flee from what approached.

The boy and the Elder were separated, and as people scattered forward, running and pushing in all directions, the boy found himself further down the road and pushed into a merchant's stall, landing in a heap.

As the boy came to one knee, with the frightened merchant of the tent huddled behind him, the crowd that ran along the road in front of the tent suddenly thinned. The boy stood and stepped toward the opening of the tent, and as he did so, an enormous, black bull with long, curved horns stormed by, only an arm's reach in front of the boy.

As the large bull passed, the boy cautiously peered out from the tent to look after the rampaging animal, screams and shouts still audible ahead of its path down the road. And in the next instant, the boy caught the sound of galloping horse's hooves on the cobblestone road, racing from the direction from which the black bull had come, as a man on a horse raced past him with rope in hand, in pursuit to gain control of the rampant bull.

After a moment more, people that had found hiding in merchant tents and stalls along the road began to reappear, and as they did, the boy stepped out into the road to search for the Elder, but to no avail. He could not be seen down either direction of the road, and the more the boy looked and the longer he did not find the Elder, he became panicked, wandering first one direction through the masses, then back, doubting if he should stay where he was or if he should continue to seek out the Elder.

Where the road widened a bit and no merchant tents or stalls stood, the boy stepped from the flow of people on the busy road and, once outside of the flow and noise of the crowd, heard a woman's voice behind him.

"Boy," the voice said.

The boy turned to see an elderly woman sitting on a wooden bench at the edge of the road. She wore an elegant dark robe and had silvery grey hair pulled neatly back, revealing a face that had seen many seasons. She held a long, smooth walking stick in one hand, and as the boy studied her, he noticed that her eyes were grey with blindness.

But despite the blindness in her eyes, the boy sensed that she somehow was indeed looking at him. She motioned for him to come to her, and the boy approached.

"Sit," she said simply, as the boy studied her clouded eyes.

"I cannot sit," said the boy, who had no idle time for the blind woman, "for I am on a journey of great importance and have lost my guide."

"I have knowledge of your guide," said the woman calmly, surprising the boy.

"Sit," she repeated, this time the boy complying.

As the boy sat next to her, she remained facing out toward the busy road as she continued.

"Indeed, your journey East is of great importance," she said, again surprising the boy with knowledge of the direction in which he journeyed.

"How do you know of it," asked the boy, "and what knowledge have you of my guide?"

"I am a Seer, from a line of Seers going back many generations," said the old blind woman. "It is why I do not need my eyes, for I have vision beyond that of the eye, and with this vision I know of what you seek. But while your heart is true, there is danger around you."

"Yes, there are perils along the journey," replied the boy. "This I have been told."

The woman bowed her head slightly and leaned toward the boy.

"I see the perils along the journey," she began softly, "but more threatening is the peril that travels with you."

The boy was confused by what she had said, and his mind drifted through the things that the Elder had said to him about what danger might lie ahead of him, as well as what perils he had already encountered along the way. Then his mind came to a startling interpretation of her words.

"The Elder?" said the boy softly, incredulous.

The old woman sat back upright next to the boy and breathed a long sigh.

"The pictures in your mind of what the journey is can be changed by what you allow inside," said the old, blind woman. "A fool's pursuit does not come from within, it is always planted there by another."

The boy went numb, and doubt and suspicion descended upon everything that the Elder had said to him about the things that they had experienced along the journey, as well as what lay ahead.

Was the traveler that came to their camp in the middle of that first night actually one that was trying to protect him from the death that awaited before him? Perhaps the Elder was a part of the group of bandits that had attacked the traveler, and was now leading the boy to them? And about this journey;

why was the boy trusting of a man, a man that he did not know, to lead him East for an unknown duration and without so much as a map, offering only the lofty assurance that all of their needs for supplies would be fulfilled along the way somehow?

The more these thoughts filled the boy's mind, the more the picture in his head made him feel that he was naïve, being taken advantage of, and being led to some horrible fate.

"It is not what I wish for you," said the old, blind woman softly, "but it is the vision of my mind, and I can do nothing but to share it with you and warn you of it."

And with that, the blind woman grasped her walking stick and used it to help rise to her feet, the boy helping her with a hand under her arm. Once to her feet, she began to tap her walking stick on the ground as she slowly started along the edge of the crowd in the road, and in a moment, she had disappeared from view.

The boy sat back down on the bench and his thoughts returned to all of the things that now seemingly did not make sense about the journey. The vision in his head grew darker and darker, and the boy could feel himself becoming more and more angry at the thought of being fooled by the Elder. And as the boy's mind raged, he was startled from his thoughts by the emergence of the Elder from the crowded road in front of him.

"I had hoped that you would wait at the edge somewhere," said the Elder with a relieved smile.

The boy's eyes were filled with anger as the Elder approached.

"Wait to do what?" snapped the boy, and he stood as the Elder reached him. "Continue on to my death?"

The Elder was stunned by the hostility in the boy, but only for an instant, then calmly replied, "To follow your Destiny Thread, to realize the Tapestry of Spirit."

"Yes, I know of the things you spoke of," retorted the boy angrily, "but I don't know if those things even exist. Perhaps they are but fool's pursuits!"

The Elder merely stood before the boy, seeing and feeling his anger, sensing his doubt and suspicion. He looked into the boy's eyes and spoke calmly.

"As I said in the beginning, it was you who summoned me. What you seek is not a fool's pursuit; it is the pursuit of truth, your truth. But as I also said in the beginning, the decision to travel this journey is yours alone. I am only here to guide you along the way. If you no longer wish to continue on this path, then I am no longer needed," said the Elder calmly, who then removed his pack and laid it on the ground next to the boy.

"It is nearly empty," said the Elder of his pack, "but will help sustain you for a while longer on your journey back to the West, if that is where you wish to return."

The boy's mind was spinning. In less than a day, he had gone from the extremes of belief in the journey he was on and the reasons for it, to belief that truth existed in none of it, and if the Elder were truly a peril to him as the old, blind woman had said, why was he so willing to allow the boy to decide if the journey East would continue?

As the boy's mind was consumed with conflicted thoughts, the Elder spoke again.

"The pictures in your mind can be changed by what you allow inside. Only you will know if you follow a fool's pursuit that has been planted by another."

And with that, the Elder turned and began walking along the crowded road toward the East, leaving the boy with both packs and a mind filled with confusion and uncertainty.

As the Elder drifted into the crowd and became lost from view, the boy's head grappled with his heart over what to do next.

With his head, the boy thought of the security of going back to the West, to things familiar and safe. Within a few days, he could be back to where he had called home, with the events of the last few days but a memory. No longer would he fear the perils of the journey that had already come to pass, or those that would be sure to follow.

But with his heart, he felt of the hope and promise that seeking his Destiny Thread brought, of meeting the Mage and realizing the Tapestry of Spirit, as he had come to understand these things, and he thought of finding the answers to his unspoken questions.

His thoughts then turned to the Elder, and how everything that he had said to the boy from the moment they met had somehow made the boy feel at ease and protected. He thought about the fact that, until meeting the old, blind woman on the bench, he had never had a reason to doubt the Elder or his intentions. It was only from the blind woman's words that the boy felt doubt and suspicion, and it surprised him suddenly to realize that his feelings could be stirred and directed by another with such apparent ease.

His final thoughts were then on the words that both the old, blind woman and the Elder had spoken, words of wisdom about what picture he had allowed to exist within his mind. They were the same words of wisdom from seemingly opposing figures, and the boy knew that he himself was the only one that could interpret them.

A clear feeling began to well up within the boy; a feeling that his journey was a journey of truth, and that his pursuits, while uncommon to the masses, were also true. The light of illumination lay before him, with the Elder at his side, while only the shadows of darkness and unanswered questions lay behind.

And with that realization, with that belief, he quickly picked up both packs and hurried off toward the East, the direction in which the Elder had gone.

After a moment of navigating the crowded road, he saw the Elder ahead of him, and his heart filled with happiness. This too—the feeling that he again felt truth and purity of the Elder and his intentions—the boy took as an important part of the picture that he not only saw in his mind, but also felt in his heart.

As he approached the Elder from the side, he held out his pack. The Elder stopped, turned to the boy, smiled, and simply took the pack and put it on his back.

The two continued East and had soon left the city.

❧ 7 ☙

By mid-afternoon, and in the open terrain of sprawling grasslands, the boy and the Elder had come to a wide river. While not very deep, its waters ran quickly, and its bottom was rocky and uneven and lined with slippery algae and plants. Across the river's width were a handful of small stones that rose above the water, just large enough to create a path for them to cross upon.

From the bank of the river, the Elder spoke.

"There is much wisdom in this crossing," said the Elder, "but only with you leading."

The boy did not understand why it was so, but nodded nonetheless, then stepped to where the small path of stones led across the river, and took a tentative step from the bank and out onto the first stone above the water.

As the Elder remained on the bank, the boy's path into the river was anything but uneventful, with several of the boy's steps along the way landing him nearly in the water, his arms whirling first one way to keep him from falling forward, then whirling the opposite way to keep him from falling back. At times, the boy would try to balance himself between stones, with one foot ahead of him on one stone, the other foot behind him on another, only to produce the same flailing to stay upright and out of the water. At other times, the boy would hop altogether from one stone, over another, and to one beyond, always landing unsurely, nearly falling.

When the boy had reached the middle of the river, the Elder shouted out to him to stop where he was. The boy did as he was told, placing both feet upon the stone beneath him, struggling to stay balanced, his arms flailing about yet again for balance as the water around him rushed by. Once balanced, the boy precariously turned in place on the stone to face the Elder.

As the boy watched, the Elder began his crossing of the river, using the same stones that the boy had chosen as his path. But unlike the boy's awkward crossing, the Elder's steps were gentle, steady, and measured. As he crossed, his arms remained at his sides, not needed for balance from flailing that did not occur.

On each stone, the Elder placed first one, then both feet, then paused and looked around at the surroundings in the river. Once he had spent a short moment consuming the surroundings from the stone on which he stood, he would step to the next one, first with one foot, then the other, again pausing once there and repeating the process of taking in his surroundings.

The Elder methodically continued in this way, and as the boy waited, he himself began to also take in his surroundings from there on his stone.

And as the boy surveyed the river from its center, he came to see the graceful beauty of the water as it flowed and swirled and moved around him: the small fish that darted here and there beneath its surface, the gentle swaying in the current of the green plants anchored to its bottom, and the simple yet somehow beautifully complex sound of the water itself as it meandered along its course.

In suddenly seeing all of these things that were lost to him when his focus was solely on getting to the other side, the boy found himself wanting to stay in the middle of the river there for a while longer, the stone upon which he stood now feeling quite steady beneath his feet.

After another moment, the Elder came to stand on the stone next to the boy's.

"Please, continue," said the Elder, to which the boy turned upon his stone, yet this time with much more calm and steadiness.

The remainder of the boy's crossing of the river was as the Elder's had been to its center, with first one foot, then the other, pausing on each stone to enjoy that which surrounded him, and over those remaining stones, the boy did not flail or lose his balance even once.

With the Elder following the boy across in the same way, they arrived together at the bank a few moments later. As the boy paused on the bank, looking out across the water that he had just crossed and thinking of the wisdom that indeed had lay within it as the Elder had said, the Elder spoke.

"Every grand journey to a desired destination usually begins with the destination in mind," he started, "but there is as much to be desired and learned from during the smaller journeys that combine in making the grand journey."

The boy understood that the one was made up of the many.

"To place your attention solely on crossing a distance will deny you the joy of taking the steps," said the Elder, looking out to the water. "For the joy is not in being on this side or that, it is in each step of the journey across."

The boy was beginning to see the Elder as the river; as one of great wisdom. The boy himself looked to the water, and in it, he saw its natural and effortless movement, from snow in the mountains, to rivers as this that crossed vast distances, to its return to the Sea.

And just as the snow in the mountains will eventually return to the Sea, the boy thought, his journey would eventually return him to the Tapestry of Spirit, as the Elder had explained.

They left the bank of the river and continued East across the green grasslands. Throughout the rest of the afternoon, the boy reflected on the journey, and he began to feel that he truly was on the only journey that mattered, the only pursuit in his young life that had ever mattered, since having been forced as a boy to live in the World of men. And although he traveled, he did not see himself as a traveler, rather a journeyer, as in the boy's mind there now existed a distinction in the World between those that simply traveled and those that truly journeyed. It was part of the wisdom of the river that had been bestowed upon him.

The boy also found himself more and more at ease in trusting his decision about the Elder, and his leading of the boy on his journey. As they sat and ate a meal, a meal that would consume the last of the provisions and leave both of their packs empty, the boy even then did not feel concern at when they would eat again. Such had his trust in the Elder, and the way of those who journeyed, grown.

It was a new feeling for the boy, one in which his trust in the outcome of things comforted him, despite the circumstances; in unfamiliar lands, completely reliant on the Elder for guidance and protection, and now, with nothing but an empty pack.

The boy was beginning to re-discover his faith in things, in himself, and in others, for while on the journey he had been tested by the darkness on several occasions, only to emerge beyond to continue his journey East. And in his re-discovery of faith in these things, the boy again felt as if a man, as he had when discussing his dream of his Muse with the Elder, feeling capable of choosing the course for his life.

And as the boy thought of the unborn seasons that waited ahead of him in his life, and of what he thought he would become if he were to find his Destiny Thread, he began to wonder about the Elder, about the life that he had led over the many seasons that he had seen.

"Have you always been a guide?" asked the boy.

"We are, each of us, all of us, both the guide and the guided as we move along our Destiny Threads," said the Elder. "I have been a guide when I have been summoned."

"As I summoned you somehow?" asked the boy.

The Elder nodded and then explained.

"I had a dream of meeting a boy in the marketplace, when the Sun was at it highest in the sky and would cast no shadows."

The boy was astonished at hearing of the Elder's dream, one in which he sought the boy, just as the boy's dream had moved him to seek the Elder. It was as the Elder had said, that dreams truly were powerful, for they reveal the truth in things, even if they are not understood at the time.

"Only I had to wait two days for your arrival," added the Elder with a grin, referring to the boy's delay in heeding the first of his two, identical dreams that would bring them together. "For you had not yet learned to regard the wisdom of your dreams."

The boy grinned back, knowing that he would always honor and never again question the power of his dreams.

And they continued East.

~ 8 ~

As the Sun behind them to the West neared the horizon, the boy and the Elder came to notice an enormous, high-arching tree in the distance ahead of them, a solitary giant standing tall out in the gently rolling green grasslands. It was an odd thing to see in the landscape, for there were no other trees of any kind in sight. And as they continued toward it, the tree's enormity continued to become clear, and it was a tree unlike any the boy had ever seen.

Its trunk, smooth and mighty, the width of ten men shoulder to shoulder the boy estimated, rose from enormous, meandering roots that radiated from the trunk at the ground, visible above the soil for some distance before turning downward and disappearing from view. As the trunk rose up toward the sky, it divided over and over into hundreds of thick branches that curved upward and outward in the most artistic manner, leading to a vast canopy of countless small leaves, high above the ground, that fluttered randomly in the late afternoon breeze.

The sight was magnificent, and the majesty of it in the fading light filled the boy with awe as he and the Elder continued toward it.

Soon, as they stepped under the edge of the vast canopy of leaves high above, with the massive trunk still thirty or forty steps ahead of them, they noticed a thin, tanned old man facing toward them as he sat on one of the mighty roots that grew from the trunk of the tree. As the boy and the Elder continued on toward him, his appearance became clearer.

He was a generation older than the Elder, with scraggly grey hair hanging down around his face, a long, grey beard reaching to the middle of his chest, and he rose as the Elder and boy approached.

With hands clasped over his heart, he greeted them.

"Welcome," he said, a warming smile across his face. "I have been expecting you," he added, which puzzled the boy, but not the Elder.

"Sit, please," said the old man, motioning them toward a place on a mighty root across from the one upon which he had been seated. As the boy and the Elder approached it, the boy noticed that its surface was smooth from wear, as if by countless others who had sat there before them.

Between the two massive roots, but further away from the tree from where they would be seated, a low, gentle fire burned.

Like a host seating his guests, the old man saw to it that they had been seated comfortably before he spoke again.

"I was just about to prepare our evening meal," said the old man, and the boy realized that his question earlier in the day about from where their next meal would come had just been answered.

And with that, the old man turned, stepped over the mighty root and around the back of the trunk of the tree, kneeling and busying himself with things near the ground that the boy could not see clearly.

The boy, seated next to the Elder on the mighty root, leaned in closely and asked quietly, "Who is that?"

"He is a great, wise Sage," replied the Elder softly.

The boy sat straight and looked toward where the thin, modest, simple old man moved about deliberately near the trunk of the tree. The boy again leaned in closely toward the Elder.

"That is a great Sage?" questioned the boy softly.

"He is one who lives his Destiny Thread, met the Mage, and returned to the Tapestry of Spirit," said the Elder.

The boy sat, incredulous, thinking to himself that what the Elder had just said to him could not be true.

Just then, the Sage returned from the base of the tree carrying three large, red-colored roots.

"Your guide speaks the truth," said the Sage affirmatively, and the boy blushed with embarrassment at his doubts being unknowingly overheard.

"I am along your journey in order to help with your understanding of what you seek, and why," said the Sage, as he stepped away from the trunk of the tree, toward the small fire, and carefully lodged the roots into the base of its flames. He then rose and stepped to the mighty root across from the boy and the Elder, the root he was seated upon when they first approached, and sat.

The boy thought for a moment of all that he had been told by the Elder while on the journey, and the things that he had seen. And while the boy's interest was still mostly on the meeting of the Mage, sitting across from the Sage—one who had actually returned to the Tapestry of Spirit—compelled him to ask of it. The boy began with a simple question.

"Does the Tapestry of Spirit hold answers?" he asked.

"It holds the truth, which can be answers to those that seek," replied the Sage.

"My truth?" asked the boy.

"One's Destiny Thread is a singular truth to the individual," explained the Sage, "but when one returns to the Tapestry of Spirit, its truth is shared by all."

The Sage paused and looked appreciatively at the attentive boy sitting across from him.

"To be so moved as to journey in search of answers to unspoken questions is to feel the distance between yourself and the Tapestry of Spirit," said the Sage. "Yet, while there are many that journey who seek, not all that travel will find, for they are bound by what they have been taught and not of what they know."

The Sage rose and stepped to the fire, knelt beside it, and using a short, crooked stick from nearby, turned the cooking roots nestled in its base.

"One will always see what is looked for," he continued, the soft light of the low fire casting a warm glow upon his face. "But the true quest is to find what is sought. It is the difference between traveling and journeying, and within this difference lies yet another difference; that between the vision of the eye, and the vision beyond that of the eye."

As the Sage rose from the fire to return to his seat across from the boy and the Elder, the boy reflected on his own similar thoughts from earlier in the day, and spoke next.

"And that," offered the boy, hoping that what he would say next would be affirmed as correct, "with vision beyond that of the eye—the vision of the heart—one is able to return to the Tapestry of Spirit?"

The Sage smiled at the growing understanding within the boy before replying.

"And once returned, you will see Spirit in all things, as it is made of us, and we are made of it, and this will never change," said the Sage.

The boy, pleased by the truth of his own insights, thought for a moment before continuing.

"My guide, as well as you, speak not of finding it, but rather of returning to it," said the boy, "and although you say that it is made of us, and we are made of it, and it has and always will be this way, I cannot recall ever being a part of it."

The Sage smiled before commencing to show the boy why it was so.

"Recall moments in your life when all the World was bright and open to you," said the Sage to the boy.

The boy's mind drifted easily to the seasons of his childhood, with frequent dreams of the Mage, and he smiled and nodded.

"Now, recall moments in your life when darkness had closed in from all around," said the Sage next.

The boy's mind was reluctantly forced to that day, the darkest day of his young life, of finding his Mother, lifeless, and how the World would forever be changed to him. How on that day, the boy within him was forced into the World of men.

But in the two seemingly opposing memories, the boy felt that they indeed held something in common, something that he could not identify yet was present in both, just below the surface of the recollections.

"It is when the clutter of the World is brushed aside that the Tapestry of Spirit is most visible," said the Sage, "and it is seen either as within the palm of your hand, or so distanced as to be nearly out of sight. It is in those times that paths and pursuits are seen anew, and with clarity of one's Destiny Thread revealed, its inclusion within the Tapestry of Spirit is clear."

The boy's curiosity turned to what the Sage's journey might have held.

"And the return to the Tapestry of Spirit?" asked the boy.

The Sage looked to him and merely smiled.

"It is the simplest of things, yet it is beyond language or art or song," he said.

While providing essentially no details, the answer from the Sage was somehow perfectly fitting, in the boy's mind.

"And of the Mage?" continued the boy.

"As your guide has shared with you," replied the Sage, "it is the Mage that enables within you the vision of the heart, and with that vision you will gain sight of the single strand from which all Destiny Threads, and therefore the Tapestry of Spirit, are spun from. It is the single strand that is common to all of these things, and it is there to guide you—your actions and your words—and in simply heeding it, you follow and live your Destiny Thread, and in so doing, you return to the Tapestry of Spirit."

The Sage paused, and then added, "The single strand is what transforms a life lived along a single Destiny Thread to a life lived within the Tapestry of Spirit among all Destiny Threads."

The boy sat in silence for a moment as he considered all that the Sage had said, and the Sage sat in patient silence for the boy's next question.

"Then to live in harmony with the single strand," the boy began, "is to enable one to live one's Destiny Thread, and in living one's Destiny Thread while in harmony of the single strand, one can see that all Destiny Threads are woven together in the Tapestry of Spirit?"

The Sage smiled broadly and nodded.

The boy reflected on the relationships between the things, all seemingly connected and made possible by the single strand of which the Sage spoke.

"For such a simple thing," the boy began, "it seems to make much possible."

"In being a simple thing," the Sage replied, "it makes all possible."

The boy waited for the Sage to continue, to identify the single strand of which all seemed to be spun, but the Sage was silent, prompting the boy to speak.

"And this single strand is?" he asked.

The Sage smiled and replied simply, "It is something that is realized truly only through experience, which meeting the Mage will reveal to you."

Being a boy as he was, the boy tried in vain to hide his disappointment at not having the answer revealed to him in that moment, but he pursed his lips in acceptance that patience would be needed, trusting that the meeting of the Mage would make all clear.

The Sage rose, stepped to the fire, and, using the short, crooked stick, rolled the three cooked roots from the base of the fire and out to the bare ground to cool, just as the boy asked another question related to his last.

"And the duration of your journey along your Destiny Thread to the meeting of the Mage?" he asked through a sly grin, hoping to at least understand how many days lay before him until reaching the answer of what the single strand was.

The Sage smiled at the boy's inquisitive ingenuity, and then replied, "It was both a lifetime and an instant," answered the Sage. "A lifetime of feeling that within," he continued, touching his hand to his heart, "there existed something that I neglected to see. An instant in that once I allowed myself to see it, the journey of the return to the Tapestry of Spirit was before me."

The answer again did little to quell the anxiousness for discovery within the boy, which again was obvious to the Sage, to which he only smiled and then offered some consolation.

"Your journey is as the river you crossed; it must happen one step at a time."

The stunned boy turned to the Elder beside him, surprised at the Sage's knowledge of the river that they had crossed, to which the Elder only smiled and offered, "As I said, he is a great, wise Sage."

By then, the roots had cooled and the Sage delivered one each to the boy and the Elder, then sat again on the mighty root across from them, his own meal in hand.

"Now, what would you like to eat?" he asked of the boy.

The boy was confused at the question, for within their hands were simple, cooked roots.

"What would you like to taste for this meal?" repeated the Sage with a smile.

The boy, then inclined to indulge the Sage, thought of what food he fancied most.

"The taste of a pie made of sweet Guava fruit," replied the boy, unabashed.

The Sage and the Elder laughed aloud.

"I would expect a boy to desire such a taste for an evening meal, and all meals for that matter," said the Sage. "So please, dine then," he said rather elegantly.

The boy looked again at the simple root within his hands and took a bite. But the root did not taste of a simple root, instead of a pie made of sweet Guava fruit, astounding the boy.

With wide eyes, the boy chewed happily on the root, and the three of them shared a meal.

Afterwards, the boy resumed his questions of the Sage.

"With your own journey East completed, why is it that you live here so simply, beneath this tree?" asked the boy.

"You hold a notion of Destiny as one defined by standards and measures," replied the Sage, "yet the only truth in one's life is their truth in following their Destiny Thread, however grand or mundane it may be perceived to be."

The boy's confused expression prompted more wisdom from the Sage.

"One's Destiny Thread winds along its course and back to the Tapestry of Spirit, like a river meandering through the landscape. The truth in one's life, therefore, is not measured by how unchanging they are in course, but rather by how true to themselves and their Destiny Thread they are through the changes of the course."

The boy reflected on his own perceptions of what a worthy Destiny would look like, suddenly realizing that to judge a Destiny is to dishonor it.

"Despite one's Destiny Thread residing within them, as it has from their birth," continued the Sage, "there is much, much toil in the World from pursuits to the contrary."

The boy was confused, and looked for clarity with a question.

"But to strive for, to sacrifice for, to toil for something that is held of value," said the boy, "that is to toil in error?"

"To toil and be lifted by it is to be in truth," replied the Sage. "But to toil and be reduced by it is to be bound by the shadows of the World. For toil that reduces is a sign of things not in balance, not in the natural state of things, and from that, suffering is born into the World."

The boy continued to struggle with the wisdom of the Sage's words, to which the Sage offered a succinct statement regarding the boy's perception of Destiny.

"Your Destiny is not what you are to be, your Destiny is what you are, for your heart beats only in this moment."

And the boy suddenly had a sense of the importance of the breath that he was about to take. The Sage continued.

"To have returned to the Tapestry of Spirit is to have returned to one's Nature. My Nature is here. But as my Destiny Thread winds to a different path and place, so shall my path and place be in the World. As the snow that falls on the mountains eventually and naturally finds its way to return to the Sea, so does a person finding a way to return to the Tapestry of Spirit. The journey cannot be forced, and in fact, there is no need to attempt it by force, as it will occur on its own. All that is needed is to allow it to happen."

It was then that the boy had an unusual thought; that perhaps, over the past several seasons of his life in the World of men, that he himself had created his distance from the Tapestry of Spirit. And it was from this unusual thought that the boy then had a profound realization.

He realized that his journey with the Elder was not leading him away from his home, but rather, it was returning him to it.

That the despair that had grown in his life over the past several seasons while in the World of men was not from a lack of ascension within the World of men, but rather from the forced pursuit to live in the World of men, which led to a distancing of himself from the Tapestry of Spirit and from his Nature. And the despair was from following pursuits that caused him to drift from who he was, from what his Nature was, which was why the Sage and the Elder referred to a 'return' to the Tapestry of Spirit.

The Sage sensed the boy's realizations, and spoke.

"The longer one is separate from themselves," he said, "the more tolerant they become of being so, and even more days will pass without truth, making any journey of return more difficult and more unlikely with each setting of the Sun. This is why I rejoice in you; that it is in your youth that you seek answers to your unspoken questions. For there are many that arrive here from the West, older than you, that cannot find the way to complete their journey."

For the first time since the boy's journey had begun, he felt that he was beginning to understand the essence of the Tapestry of Spirit. And as the boy thought of the past several seasons of his life, and the elusive answers to his unspoken questions, he realized that what he unknowingly sought was indeed a return to the Tapestry of Spirit.

"So, to answer your question," replied the Sage, "I am here, beneath this great, curved tree, because I am living my Destiny Thread, and as such, I am in balance with my Nature. And it is my Nature, at this point in my Destiny Thread, to be here to meet those who travel East so that I may humbly share of my wisdom. It is not one's surroundings that dictate one's truth, it is one's truth that enables one to find their natural surroundings."

The boy thought deeply on the Sage's truth, and that in living it, he was in his Nature.

"As for this tree," the Sage continued, "you may only see it as but a tree, but this tree is the Tapestry of Spirit lived."

The boy looked upward to all of the simple beauty that the tree appeared to be, yet did not understand that it could be so much more than that as the Sage had just claimed.

"This tree is of the Tapestry of Spirit?" the boy asked, returning his gaze to the Sage.

"Indeed" replied the Sage. "Those that merely travel by this tree will only see a tree, believing nothing of note or consequence happens from it. But those that truly journey by this tree will see the wondrous things that it displays."

The Sage leaned back and looked upward into the spanning mass of the tree across the darkening sky, the boy doing likewise.

"With each passing of the Sun," continued the Sage, "it grows slightly more, its leaves whisper and dance in the breeze, and as its mighty trunk sways, it sounds its song to the World. Its great curved branches are as Destiny Threads, weaving their own way individually, yet all a part of the great tree itself, woven together, with each part in harmony that it lives as itself, but also with others."

As the boy looked up with the Sage into all of the beauty that he described, the boy himself began to see the tree as the Sage spoke of it.

"From the tips of the smallest of its roots, deep into the soil of the World, to the tips of the highest leaves up in the sky above, the Tapestry of Spirit as it exists in Nature is present, standing as a monument for the World of men to follow," said the Sage.

The boy started to become lost in all of the intricacies that were now displayed above him in the wonder that was the tree.

"Once you have returned to the Tapestry of Spirit," continued the Sage, "you will see that it is everywhere, for this is the way of Nature, and Nature is a constant reminder of balance by being in balance, and as such, will return things to balance, as it is the cycle of things in the World."

The Sage lowered his gaze from the tree to rest on the boy.

"Yet the World of men is not in balance, and while there is chaos and despair, cruelty and greed, and suffering of man at the hands of man, the Tapestry of Spirit remains tattered, for it reveals the condition of the World of men."

The boy lowered his eyes from the canopy of the tree, the past several seasons of his life as a boy among the World of men a harsh testament to the truth of the Sage's words.

"That as more drift from it, their Destiny Threads, and the single strand from which they all are spun, the Tapestry unravels and is pulled apart," the Sage explained. "But as more seek their Destiny Threads and the single strand from which all are spun, and more guides such as yours are called by the World for meetings of the Mage, the Tapestry of Spirit becomes restored toward wholeness, as it was when first woven. And as the Tapestry of Spirit becomes restored, the

World of men approaches balance, just as Nature exists, and from this, there is healing for the suffering in the World. It is this way across all tribes and clans across all the lands of the World."

The boy was profoundly moved by the words of the Sage, and imagined such beauty in the World if only suffering of man at the hands of man could end.

As the boy watched, the Sage became deeply thoughtful for a moment before speaking again, and when he spoke, it was differently than he had done up to that moment. When he spoke next, he spoke in sadness.

"The World of men—those who would presume to speak of things greater than themselves, yet never ventured to find— will forever portray an inappropriate approach by intellect to the answer of the single, unspoken question."

The boy knew of the question that the Sage spoke of. It was the question that was convoluted and contorted upon itself, one that had grown within him over the past several seasons, and one that had indeed driven the boy along the journey.

The question was one of life's meaning and reason.

Several moments more were spent in silence before they resumed conversing, but of his last statement, the Sage spoke no more, and the boy did not ask.

It was late into the evening when their discussions finally ended, and as the flames of the small fire gave way to only glowing embers, the three of them lay down to sleep, with each of them nestled into one of the many natural cradles that the tree offered at its base, where its giant roots first radiated from the mighty trunk and ran above the soil for a ways before disappearing.

As the boy settled in, leaned up against the great tree's trunk with a massive root to either side of him, he looked upward at the expansive canopy of leaves high above. In the dark sky, he noticed that the stars in the sky beyond the canopy above shone through the small gaps between the leaves, making it appear as if the stars themselves hung from the high branches of the tree.

And as the boy marveled at the tree of stars, the air brought a sweet scent to him, a scent reminiscent, for some reason, of fond times as a boy spent in the marketplace with his Mother. It was with that fondness in his heart that the boy closed his eyes and drifted off to sleep.

The following morning, the boy awoke in what seemed to be precisely the same position in which he had laid down the prior night. There, in the natural cradle of the tree and its roots, he again looked up to the canopy of the tree high above to see the first light from the rising Sun as it gently brightened its leaves. And in that moment, the boy felt a great connection to the mighty tree, for beneath it, the prior day had ended, and now a new day had begun.

The boy had slept quite peacefully and comfortably the entire night, having no memory of stirring even once. Despite having slept on the bare ground and against the hard tree, the boy's body did not ache. Despite the coldness of the morning air that surrounded him, he felt warm. And despite the usual morning hunger in his stomach upon wakening, he felt nourished.

The boy sat up and looked out to the rolling hills around him, and felt a peace, a calm, and a contentment that had a very quieting effect upon him.

The Elder and the Sage had already risen and were a few paces away, near the base of the tree. The boy rose and stepped around the trunk of the great tree, over two of the massive roots as he went, to find the Elder filling their empty packs with various roots and tubers that the soil around the tree had yielded, while the Sage appeared to be busy somehow with one of their water skins near the base of the tree.

As the boy reached them, he noticed a single, gentle trickle of water descending from the heights of the tree along its smooth trunk, a trickle that made its way from the canopy high above and down, to finally collect in a small natural basin in the ground near the base of the tree. It was against this gentle trickle of water, as it ran down the trunk of the tree, that the Sage held the mouth of one of their water skins, slowly filling it.

Upon the boy approaching, the Sage smiled and greeted the boy, "I trust you slept well?"

"Yes, very well," replied the boy, intrigued by the supply of water that the tree brought them.

"Each morning, from the dew that collects above," explained the Sage, "the leaves send water down to sustain me and those in my company."

It was yet again just as the Elder had said, that along the journey their needs would be met, and the boy was very taken with how the mighty tree so gently nurtured the Sage and he and the Elder on that morning.

With the packs of the boy and the Elder filled, the Sage prepared a morning meal, again of roots cooked in the base of the small fire. And again, the boy chose to taste of pie made of the sweet Guava fruit, which he did, enjoying it as much as the meal from the prior evening.

After eating, the boy and the Elder prepared to leave, and the Sage stood before the boy to speak.

"There will be another along your journey, one that will help with more of what you seek to understand," he said. "Where I have shown you the way of the one, she will show you the way of the many, for a single candle in the darkness will give vision to the one, but ten thousand candles can begin to bring light to the World."

The Sage placed a hand upon the boy's shoulder and offered his final wisdom.

"To be in search of answers to unspoken questions is all that is needed of you now, as a seed planted at dusk does not yield a tree by dawn. And while your journey East is perilous, it will ask only a single, simple thing of you."

The boy looked to the Sage for what it was, and the Sage spoke.

"Just be."

And with that, the boy and the Elder departed toward the East, where mountains could be seen in the distance ahead of them. And as the Sage and the mighty tree grew distant behind them, the boy thought very differently on how the Sage lived there under the mighty, curved tree.

During their travels that morning, the boy expressed to the Elder how well he felt when he awoke.

"The Tapestry of Spirit not only nourishes those that live within it, but also those who are around those that live within it," said the Elder.

The boy also shared with the Elder how his mind was filled with less and less of the doubts and worries about the journey that had existed at its start. How at the beginning of the journey, the boy admitted that he felt longing for the things that he had left behind, and their familiarity, even though they did nothing to provide answers to the unspoken questions within him.

But now, at this point in the journey, the boy thought less and less about those things, and more about the things that his Destiny Thread, the Mage, and the Tapestry of Spirit would reveal to him.

"As if, in the beginning, you may have felt that you pushed yourself away from the familiar, but now find yourself more drawn by the unfamiliar?" asked the Elder, smiling. "But ponder this—given that you are, and always will be of the Tapestry of Spirit, perhaps you are in fact now finding yourself more drawn by that which is actually familiar, just forgotten over the seasons?"

And the boy thought again of what the Sage had said, of how mountain snow naturally returns to the Sea.

Just before mid-day, they stopped and ate a meal, but try as the boy might to taste of the pie made of sweet Guava fruit, he was unable to, and he concluded that it was because of his distance from the Tapestry of Spirit that lived within the Sage.

It was early afternoon when the landscape rose gently up before them and the boy and the Elder came upon a small knoll, beyond which they could hear the sound of rushing water. As they crested the small hill, they saw before them a great river, wider than the one they had crossed only the day before, running faster and deeper. And beyond the river and in the distance, a broad mountain range rose up above the landscape from the North, stretched to the East ahead of them, then continued on toward the South.

From atop the small knoll, they could see that the wide river came from the North, then split and flowed for a distance, to then rejoin to the South. This split in the river created an isolated island of sorts in the middle of the rushing water, and on the small island of land stood a large pile of soil, next to which was a large pit, the depth of which the boy and the Elder could not see from where they stood.

As they descended the small hill to the bank of the river, the river's width and speed became clear, and the Elder could sense the anxiety in the boy, as the boy did not know how to swim. With the river's depth, there would be no stones above its surface as a path across, which meant that the boy would need to cross by entering the water.

"We will enter together, and cross on our backs," comforted the Elder, "and I will pull you across by your pack. Just remain calm and trust that I will protect you."

The boy nodded, his mouth dry, and with that, the Elder led the boy into the river.

As they entered the edge of water, the boy soon felt the pull of the powerful, cold water upon his legs. When they were waist deep, with the boy struggling to stay upright, the Elder turned him to face the bank that they had just stepped from and instructed him to cross his arms on his chest and hold the straps of his pack.

"Ready?" asked the Elder, close to the boy's ear so as to be heard over the noise of the water.

The unnerved boy nodded, still facing the bank from which they had come.

"Remember, I will keep you safe," reminded the Elder. "Remain calm in the water as I pull us across."

And with that, the boy felt himself suddenly afloat in the water, but not swept downstream, rather pulled across by the Elder just as he had promised.

It was all that the boy could do to control his panicked urge to flail as the strong, undulating water lapped at him as his bobbing body was tugged across the river by the Elder's grasp on the pack upon his back. But it seemed no sooner had they begun the crossing than the boy again felt the rocks of the river's bottom beneath his feet, and he and the Elder emerged from the chilling water and onto the bank of the island at its center.

Despite the short duration of the crossing, the cold water and the boy's panic had left him breathless. The Elder allowed him a moment to regain himself, and when the boy's smile had returned, they proceeded.

As they made their way across the small island at the center of the split river, their path took them by the large pile of soil and the deep pit beside it. As they approached, hurled soil flew up from the pit to land on the enormous pile beside it, startling them both. The Elder cautioned the boy, and they slowly stepped to the edge, hearing what lie within—a man's murmuring—before having sight of its origin.

They reached the pit, and upon looking over its edge and into its depths some two men's height below them, they saw a dirty, emaciated man, feverishly digging at its bottom with his bare hands. They could not make out the words that he said, but it appeared that he was rambling on to himself, alone there in the bottom of the pit.

"Greetings," said the Elder loudly, his hands cupped around his mouth to amplify his voice.

This startled the man in the pit and caused him to fall backward against its sides as he looked up toward them. After eyeing both the Elder and the boy next to him, the man in the pit started to scamper up its sides, nearly on his hands and knees as he crawled upward, flinging soil behind him and back down into the pit as he clamored his way toward the top.

As the man made his way up the side of the pit, the Elder and the boy stood back from its edge, and in a moment, the man had emerged and stood before them.

He was the dirtiest person that the boy had ever seen. He wore ragged, filthy clothing, and there was hardly any uncovered skin on his thin body that was not dark from soil, with only the whites of his jittery eyes true of color. Yet for all of his appearance, he seemed oblivious to it.

"What brings you here?" he asked bluntly, his words revealing crooked and discolored teeth, his eyes darting in a crazed fashion between the Elder and the boy.

"We journey East," said the Elder, looking to the boy. "A journey of great importance."

The crazed man became very interested suddenly and fidgeted a bit, and despite their isolation in the middle of the terrain, in the middle of the rushing river, and enveloped by the loudness of the moving water on all sides, he leaned in toward the boy as if to keep secret what he would say next.

"In search of the ore?" he asked suspiciously, eyeing first the boy, then the Elder, and then the boy again.

The Elder and the boy looked to each other. They both knew of the ore of which the crazed man spoke; a beautiful, swirled mixture of both silver and gold that was much heavier and more valuable than any other known ore.

"We seek no such thing," replied the Elder, drawing the sharp stare of the man for a moment, only then for it to jump to the boy, and then back to the Elder again, the crazed man's frenzied eyes stirring concern in both of them.

"Well," started the crazed man defiantly, "if you were, this land would not yield it."

"So, you dig for ore yourself?" asked the boy innocently.

"Yes!" replied the crazed man, giddy happiness flashing across his face for an instant, only then to be quickly wiped from his features, with some effort on his part.

"No!" he then blurted hurriedly, unconvincingly, followed with, "but if I was in search of it, I would not search here!"

His suspicious gaze returned to the boy, then to the Elder, then to the boy again, and it was very clear to both the Elder and the boy that some immediate distance from the crazed man would be wise.

"We are only here to rest during our crossing of the river, and now will continue on toward the East," assured the Elder, and he nudged the boy to the side along the edge of the pit, careful to remain facing the crazed man and keeping himself between him and the boy.

As the Elder continued to shuffle himself and the boy around the edge of the pit and toward the river beyond, the crazed man continued to position himself so as to always be between the pit and his unwanted visitors.

The man did not say another word to them.

The Elder and the boy reached the other branch of the river, and in preparing to enter its waters again, the Elder waved back to the man, who only stood motionless where they had left him in front of his pit.

The boy, more afraid then of the crazed man than of the second crossing of the water, led the Elder into the water and turned as he had done before when the water was at his waist. And as before, the Elder grasped the boy's pack from behind and pulled him across the river, the duration of which no longer a concern to the boy as it had been on the first crossing only moments before.

Once on the bank, the Elder and the boy turned back toward the man on the island, who had remained standing where he was, in front of his pit, watching them as they made the crossing.

Satisfied that the Elder and the boy were no longer in his domain, the man stepped over the edge of the pit and was out of sight in its depths.

And as the boy and the Elder stood on the bank of the river, the boy was grateful for the warmth of the Sun, and to be off of the island with the crazed man.

"I wonder if he will ever find the ore there," asked the boy aloud, and then thought that even if the crazed man did, he would have no way of getting it across the river.

ᔐ 10 ᔐ

By late afternoon, the journey East had led the Elder and the boy into the sloping foothills of the surrounding mountains. They found themselves on a traveled path, and soon the path began ascending steeply into the mountains. Before long, the path had narrowed to not more than a precarious footpath, with one side blending to the steep mountainside, the other a sheer edge falling dangerously away.

And on this footpath they climbed higher and higher, and along the way, passed a man coming down from the mountains, a man leading two packed mules behind him. With a greeting exchanged, they carefully passed the man and his mules, and then continued the climb.

In need of a meal and a rest in the rapidly thinning air, the boy and the Elder found a part of the path that had widened, just enough for a few of the already scarce bushes among the altitudes of the mountains to grow along the outer edge of the path.

As they sat with their backs against the rocky mountainside and ate, a tiny, shimmering bird suddenly appeared and whirred in to hover an arm's length from the boy's face, startling him.

The boy had never seen a bird of its kind, or anything similar, and was mesmerized. As it hovered before the boy's eyes, master of the air around it, its shimmering blue, green, and red feathers brilliant in the Sun, it turned its small head as if studying the boy, revealing a long, slender beak.

"It is a Colibri," said the Elder softly as the bird hung before the boy's eyes. "As it hovers and feeds from one flower to the next, it spreads the life of the flowers from one to the next."

The boy continued to marvel at it, not sure of what amazed him more: that the colorful bird could float in the air as it was, or that it seemed to be studying him.

"It is a sacred and meaningful bird to the people of this region," continued the Elder, "for as it journeys, it brings new life. But I know not of what it does at this height, for there are little flowering plants here," added the Elder curiously.

As the boy continued to study the bird hovering before him, it suddenly flew away from the boy's face and dropped down to near the base of one of the small bushes along the outer edge of the path and resumed hovering there, looking back toward the boy for a moment. Then, as soon as it had come, the bird darted up over the bush and then down into the depths of the sloping mountainside beyond it, and was gone.

The boy looked to the Elder and smiled, then returned his gaze to the bush across from him where the bird was last seen, and as his gaze fell to the bush, something shiny within its tangled base caught the boy's eye.

The boy rose and stepped to the bush, kneeling and carefully working his hand and arm in toward the shiny object, careful not to lose his balance and fall over the edge and down the steep mountainside.

His fingers touched something not of the bush, and when he gently withdrew his arm, he held a small metal figurine on an open string of leather. The figurine was of silver, and was a likeness of the small bird that had just appeared before them. As the boy looked upon it in the palm of his hand, it was the most precious thing he had held in his short life, having come from a simple and poor background.

The boy stood as the Elder approached.

"Your Destiny Thread has crossed another," said the Elder.

The boy's thoughts drifted to the wisdom shared by the Sage, about Nature setting things in motion to restore balance to the World. The boy wondered if indeed his Destiny Thread had crossed another, as the Elder had just spoken of, and if the crossing would restore balance to the World somewhere because of it.

"Its meaning will make itself known when it is time," added the Elder.

The boy placed the silver figurine and its string of leather securely in his pack, then he and the Elder continued their journey, higher and higher along the narrow mountain path as the Sun sank lower and lower in the sky behind them, and the ever-thinning air continued to chill.

Soon, they passed another man, this one with only a single packed mule descending on the trail, and shortly thereafter, with the boy and the Elder mid-way to the snow-covered mountain peak that lie ahead of them to the East, they reached a small village nestled into the side of the mountain.

It was not much more than a flattening and a great widening of the path, on which were small, simple mud and stone cottages, no more than two dozen of them in total. The mountain pass reached the village, then ran through its center, in which were a few merchants and their tables selling rare mountain roots and a variety of woven items.

From the large number of mules visible in the village, as well as those that they had passed on the trail during their ascension, the boy concluded that the village was one of mostly trade, likely having something native of value that was exchanged and bartered for with those that lived below the mountain.

As the boy and the Elder entered the small village, there were only a handful of people here and there, but ahead of them on the widened path, they noticed a woman that plodded along toward them. As they neared her, they saw that she carried a small, folded, ornate tapestry. But as lively and vibrant as the colors and images were on the tapestry, the woman was not.

Although only twice the boy's age or so, she walked as though she were very, very old, with more of a shuffle of despair than a typical gait. With her gaze lowered and mindless on the ground in front of her, the boy wondered if she was even aware of his and the Elder's approach.

As the Elder and the boy passed her, the slightest glint caught the boy's eyes, but it was another two steps before the boy realized what it was, and his eyes then suddenly widened in recognition.

He stopped abruptly and removed his pack, searching within its contents as the Elder stood nearby, and after a moment, withdrew his arm and stepped quickly after the plodding woman, the Elder following.

As the boy reached the woman, he gently tapped her on the shoulder, to which she paused, and then turned tiredly to face the boy. And as her eyes met his, the boy saw a deep sadness within them, heavy and without hope. The sadness in the woman's eyes deeply moved him, and while he did not know the reason for her despair, he sensed that it had been despair endured over many seasons.

Unsure of what to say, the boy could only extend his open hand, which held the silver figurine of the Colibri bird on its leather string that he had found on the mountain trail—a figurine and string that matched the one around the woman's neck.

At the sight of it, the woman became very emotional, the tapestry dropping from her hands and opening as it reached the ground. She extended trembling hands to hold the boy's hand and its contents, and she started to weep.

And it was then that the boy indeed knew that he and the woman were to meet for some reason, that it was her Destiny Thread that was meant to cross his, as the Elder had said would happen.

"Javell," managed the woman through her tears, "my Javell," as she continued to hold the boy's hand in hers, looking to the silver figurine within. With pleading eyes, she looked to the boy, and it was clear to him what she was asking for.

The boy nodded, and the woman took the figurine on the leather string into her hands, feeling its entirety with the tips of her trembling fingers, managing through her cries again what she had said a moment before.

"My Javell," she repeated, "my dearest Javell."

She then held the silver figurine to her heart, nearby to the one that she wore, and she continued to weep.

Several people within the village approached at the scene, and the woman showed them the silver figurine and then looked to the silent boy. And with the unspoken explanation by the woman, the villagers all knew of the silver figurine's meaning to her, and they embraced her lovingly, and looked fondly to the boy.

After another moment, the woman was able to speak.

"How did you come by this?" she asked the boy.

"It was entangled in a bush on the side of the trail, a half day's journey down the mountain from here," he said.

The somber woman nodded slowly, as she again held the small figurine in her fingertips, rubbing its surface gently as if hoping to somehow bring it to life.

"A Mother knows," she said sadly, "for there is a bond between Mother and child like no other."

The woman's words surfaced memories within the boy of his own Mother, and the connection that existed between them.

The woman again looked up to the boy, this time with eyes that looked deeply into his, as if in deep contemplation about their meeting. After a moment, she spoke.

"There is something that must be passed," she said, and motioned toward the village.

The boy picked up the tapestry that the woman had dropped to the ground, and held it gently in his hands. And with that, the woman led them into the village a short distance and to a small cottage, as the light of the setting Sun began to withdraw from the mountain sky above.

Once inside the cottage, the woman lit a lantern, and the boy and the Elder could then see the small, scant room more clearly. Along one wall were two small mattresses of straw, end to end. Across from them and in one corner stood a small wooden table, two wooden chairs beside it, to which the woman motioned. The boy sat, but the Elder remained standing nearby. The woman placed the lantern upon the table and sat in the other chair beside the boy, holding the small, silver figurine in her hands, her fingers again rubbing its surface as her mind drifted to seasons past. The soft light from the lantern lit the silver figurine that she herself wore, making it as brilliant as the actual Colibri bird itself had been, hovering before the boy in the light of the Sun earlier that day.

"You have returned my boy Javell to me," she said finally, looking up to the boy with deep gratitude, before returning her gaze to the figurine in her hands.

"It was many seasons ago when he was lost on the mountain," she began, "returning from trading in the village a day down the mountain. But only the mule he traveled with returned, still packed with its goods."

The woman looked up to the boy, managed something of a smile, and said, "He was about your age," her gaze then returning to the precious object in her hands. "He was never found, but I knew," said the woman, looking again to the boy, tears welling up in her eyes.

The boy could not imagine the agony of her life, from one day to the next, over the seasons of uncertainty since her son was lost. To have lived since then, with no desire for each day as it came, must surely have been an end of life in itself.

"A season before he was lost," continued the woman, distant memories returning to her, "a lone woman, young as I was then, journeyed on the path through these mountains and to this village. It was something unseen, a woman in such a perilous region alone, yet she was quite capable it seemed to me. With the dark of night approaching, I offered her a bed, which she was grateful for."

The Elder and the boy sat in silence as they listened to the woman continue.

"And after a meal that evening, she spoke of the most wonderful things—of Destiny and of Spirit."

The woman smiled, as if back to that night, "and these things gave great happiness to my young Javell," she said.

And with her smile came tears again, and as she looked to the boy, he saw that they were tears of happiness from that night so many seasons past.

"She wore a silver figure such as this, on a leather string," continued the woman, her gaze returning to the item that she held in her hands. "And with the rising of the Sun the next morning, she had gone, before either Javell or I had awoken. But left behind were two silver figures of the same, and from that day forward, both Javell and I wore them as a memory of the happiness and bright wisdom that was shared that evening by the lone woman who traveled the World."

She studied the silver figurine fondly for a moment more, and then looked to the boy.

"It has been many seasons that I have hoped for some sign of my son," she said, reaching a warm hand out and taking the boy's in hers.

As grateful as the woman before him felt, the boy felt even more so: grateful for the gift that he himself had so unwittingly just given to her. He thought about the thread of things that led to that moment, starting with the Colibri bird floating before his eyes as he and the Elder rested on the mountain trail. It was as both the Sage and the Elder had said, that Nature puts things into balance, and he knew in his heart that he had just been a part of that return to harmony. And in the instant of that realization by the boy, he felt differently. A rush of warmth filled his body as the woman held his hand in hers, and he felt what he believed to be the Tapestry of Spirit.

With a gentle squeeze of the boy's hand, the woman stood, stepping to a small, wooden chest in the corner of the room, which she opened and began to search within. A moment later, she returned with something in her hand. She sat, then placed a large, silver key on the table in front of the boy.

"When my son was just a young boy, we traveled down the mountain together for the first time," she started. "At its base, we crossed a stream, and as we crossed, he noticed a glint beneath the water's surface. It was this key," she said, pushing the key to the boy, who took it in his hands and inspected it. It was quite a large key, and he could not imagine how it could elude someone's possession.

"We did not know where or from whom it came, so we waited by the stream for a while longer, but no one returned in search of it," she explained. "During the journey back to our village, I told my son a tale about the key that we then carried with us," said the woman, her eyes becoming alive again in the memory of the experience.

"That it would be very important to someone somewhere, as keys are for locks, and locks are meant to keep precious and valuable things from the World. And in our passing of the key to another, it could be used to free something beautiful, to return it to the World. Although we did not know at the time who to give the key to, I told my son that in time, the answer would make itself known, and that the key had found its way to us so that one day, we could pass it to another."

The woman reached out and again took the boy's hand in hers.

"And now, with the beauty of my son that you have returned to me, I see that it is you who are the next to carry the key," she said.

The boy smiled and looked to the Elder, who simply nodded and smiled back.

"We journey East," said the boy, "my Elder guides me along the way."

"Then with hope, the key you will carry will somehow find its lock," said the woman, smiling. "But East from here the mountains become treacherous, with very few traveling beyond this village," said the woman, to which the Elder nodded in acknowledgement. "Please, rest here tonight, and in the morning I will prepare a meal before your passage of the mountains."

The boy and Elder agreed, and they spent the evening together talking of the woman's son and of the boy's journey, and by the end of the evening, the woman was a different person to the boy. No longer was she a slumped soul living in despair over a loss from the past. That night, with her son's memories alive in the air, she was a woman with contentment and peace in her heart, and with new hope for days ahead with meaning.

The next morning, they shared a meal at the table in the small cottage, and afterwards, as the Elder and the boy stepped from the cottage with the key securely at the bottom of the boy's pack, the boy noticed a brightness in the woman's eyes, a brightness born from a new day. The boy felt a great connection to the woman for the change within her that he had been a part of.

They parted ways and the Elder and the boy walked through the small village and out onto the trail that continued its path East and upward into the mountains. Soon, the village was out of sight behind them.

"Just like the Colibri," said the Elder, "you have given her new life."

The boy smiled, feeling himself a part of Nature that had returned balance to her.

"We all carry keys of one sort or another," said the Elder, "to both ourselves as well as to others. Keys that open the unjust locks that we allow within our Spirit, and once opened, we free the beauty that each of us carries so that it can be shared with the World."

❧ 11 ❧

Throughout the rest of the morning, the Elder and the boy continued their Easterly ascension up the narrow mountain trail, resting frequently from their growing fatigue caused by the continually thinning, cooling air.

By mid-day, they had reached an altitude where the mountain pass was cold, snowy terrain, their breath visible with each labored step. Soon, a light snow began to fall, occasionally being whipped about by frigid winds that had arisen from the mountain peaks.

At one point, the pass narrowed, straightened, and stretched out ahead of them, leading them toward a dark, ominous gash that existed in the mountainside. The shivering boy nervously surveyed the surrounding mountainside—steep, impassable, and snow-covered—and concluded that they must surely be near the apex of the mountain that lay before them.

As they followed the narrow pass that led to the dark cavern, the boy stopped, overcome with a sense of foreboding, of fear. The Elder sensed the apprehension in the boy behind him.

"It is the only way forward," said the Elder, shouting over the wind, which by then had grown to an undulating howl. The boy again looked at the steep mountainous terrain above and around the dark passageway, and knew that the Elder spoke the truth.

They continued up the trail, and as they reached the shadowy opening, the Elder stopped and stepped to the side.

"You must be the first to enter," he shouted to the boy.

The nervous boy looked to the Elder, and after a deep breath to collect his courage, he stepped passed him and into the darkness of the passageway, the Elder stepping in after him.

Whereas the pass outside the slit in the mountain was cold and windy, the inside of the passageway had a dead, quiet iciness to it, with a coldness that somehow exceeded that of the outside. To the boy, the belly of the mountain was far more cold and threatening than the pass outside.

As the boy's eyes adjusted to the darkness, he was able to make out a faint light on the other side of the passageway in the distance ahead of him, a light which he knew came from the pass as it emerged from the mountain on the other side.

But despite his goal lit in the distance ahead of him, and a relative course toward it clear in the boy's mind, the fear that he felt at crossing the darkness to reach it was as if a presence all its own within him: an uninvited and dark stranger to deny him of what he sought.

The boy's legs simply did not want to move forward and into the darkness, but in feeling the Elder's firm, supportive hand placed upon his shoulder, the boy summoned the strength to begin the crossing.

As the boy led the Elder on the first few unsteady steps, the passageway leveled out and the din of the howling wind outside faded.

After a dozen steps, the only sound in the darkness was that of their steps on the darkened, rocky path, along with their labored breathing. And with those many steps, the light from the opening behind them began to fade, leaving them in even more darkness. But with the Elder's hand still on the boy's shoulder, the boy kept his eyes on the faint light at the other side of the passageway across the dark distance.

As they continued forward, cautious step by cautious step, the light from the opening behind them now no longer able to illuminate anything of the path, indiscernible sounds began to rise within the passageway.

As the boy first heard them, he stopped abruptly, his breath quickening, and he listened.

At first, there were only pieces of sounds, but as the boy listened, there were more and more, overlapped on each other in an increasingly grotesque mix.

"What is that?" the frightened boy asked of the Elder behind him, his voice suddenly loud in the relative silence of the traverse.

There was no reply from the Elder, but the boy felt the Elder's hand squeeze his shoulder.

Panic rose within the boy, and it clawed at him to withdraw from the dark passage with haste, back toward the light from the path near the entrance to the passageway. But in turning to do so, the boy saw moving shadows behind he and the Elder, shadows that quickly converged to completely block all light from where they had come.

The boy quickly turned back around and saw that the same was happening to the faint light in the distance ahead of them, that shadows were coalescing into one another to block all light from the way out ahead as well.

Panic quickly gave in to terror, and as the boy stood in complete, cold blackness, his breath coming only in gasps, the sounds in the dark passageway continued to grow. They were still a jumble of sounds, but now it was clear to the boy that they were pieces of voices, dark voices, voices that said things that the boy could not understand, yet filled him with fear, despair, and doubt. And as the boy stood, frozen in terror, he was consumed with a feeling of utter hopelessness. Without being able to understand what the voices were uttering, he had succumbed to their dark intent.

And motionless as he was, the boy felt the sting of a different sort of iciness moving into his body, from the outside and toward his core, leaving behind only numb, lifeless extremities, the boy's fears inexplicably convincing him that he was being turned to stone.

Soon, the dark pieces of voices had grown to drown out even the sound of the boy's frantic panting and his heartbeat within his ears, and as he felt that all light and warmth from his body would soon be smothered out, extinguished, he felt the Elder's hand on his shoulder give another firm squeeze. And although the noise in the boy's head was deafening, what the Elder would say next from beside him was calm and somehow inexplicably clear in the boy's ears.

"In times of darkness, a course of truth together with conviction will reveal purpose, and purpose will illuminate the way."

This shook the boy from the grip of his terror, and the words of the Elder offered his mind with a way forward. Although they stood in complete darkness, the boy realized that his eyes were still wide open, and upon closing them, the boy turned his mind to listening to the words of the Elder, the sounds of them recurring in his head instead of the sounds of the dark voices. As the boy repeated the words to himself, he willed the Elder's words to put down the voices, to overcome them and banish them from his thoughts and from his will.

And as the boy sensed the slightest of retreats of the dark voices in his head, and as he repeated the words of the Elder over and over to himself, with his eyes still closed tightly in the passageway void of light, he thought again of his desire to seek and live his Destiny Thread, his journey to meet the Mage that he had dreamt of since being a boy, and of realizing the Tapestry of Spirit. The boy, through his own intention, fought for and re-discovered his course of truth.

As the sounds of the dark voices continued to subside into whispers, the boy opened his eyes, newfound courage and conviction in his heart. And with this, in the distance, the boy could see the dark shadows slowly parting to reveal the light of the other side of the passageway. And as the boy's strength grew, the faint light from the other side of the passageway slowly grew and stretched toward he and the Elder, eventually reaching their feet on the stone pass.

The way to the other side of the passageway had been illuminated. It was as the Elder had said to him only a moment prior.

With a clear course in his mind, and conviction returned to his heart, the boy resumed his steps toward the light of the pass ahead, the Elder behind him with his hand still firmly upon the boy's shoulder. And with each step, the sound of the dark whispers continued to subside and withdraw, until eventually, with the outside light of the passageway only a dozen steps away, they had disappeared completely, once again leaving the boy's ears with only the sounds of their steps on the stone path, and the breaths within their chests.

As they approached the opening of the pass to the other side of the mountain, the shivering boy was oddly greeted with warmth in the air. There was no wind howling, only the beckoning light and warmth of the pass beyond the opening.

The boy and the Elder stepped from the passageway and into the calm and warmth of a cloudless, Sun-lit day, as if the two sides of the mountain were on different sides of the World itself, so different was the feel.

The Elder removed his hand from the boy's shoulder, and turned the boy to face him.

"At times along your journey of living your Destiny Thread, you may again encounter Passageways of Shadows that stand between you and the Tapestry of Spirit," said the Elder. "But if your course is true to your heart, you will always find the strength to navigate its darkness."

It was with that statement by the Elder that the boy realized that he had had another brush with the dark shadows of the journey, and as they sat in the light and warmth of the Sun outside of the passageway and ate a meal, the boy felt somehow as if he had crossed the border that separated the West from the East.

❧ 12 ❧

The rest of the day was spent descending the Eastern side of the mountains in the warm, calm air, leaving the altitude for the lower lands, with green returning to the terrain and the pass as they journeyed.

Once at the base of the mountains, they stopped again to rest and eat. As the boy sat, he noticed above him, high in the clear blue sky, a circling black bird, and wondered if it was a vestige of the shadows from the passageway, sent to pursue him.

But something in the boy had changed with his traverse of the Passageway of Shadows. While the bird above, if yet another dark shadow, was a concern, it did not represent something that the boy felt was invincible. If the black bird above were indeed to be another dark shadow with evil intentions toward the boy, so be it. The boy would face them, as he had done several times now on the journey, and he had belief that he would again overcome them to continue his journey East.

As the boy's heart was filled with this new courage and hope for continuing his journey along his Destiny Thread to meet the Mage, the black bird turned and flew out of sight.

By late afternoon, with the mountains some distance behind them in the West, they found themselves in rolling, green, sparse grasslands. Ahead of them to the East, a small thread of smoke rose lazily in the fading light of the day, and within moments, the boy and the Elder had come upon a small clearing. In the middle of the clearing burned a small cooking fire, and around the fire sat an older woman and a young girl who both rose upon the approach of the Elder and the boy.

As the boy and the Elder reached them, the Elder simply smiled at the older woman, and she smiled back at him, and after a short moment, the Elder spoke.

"Greetings," said the Elder, the smile still across his features, as he and the boy bowed to them.

"Greetings," replied the Elder Woman, equally as friendly, and she and the girl bowed in return.

The two Elders simply stood before each other and smiled, taking each other in, it seemed to the boy.

"It has been many seasons," said the boy's Elder to the Elder Woman, the comment surprising the boy, and the girl as well.

"It has," replied the Elder Woman, and the four of them sat around the small fire.

As the two Elders began conversing between themselves, sharing of seasons spent since they were last together, the boy's gaze could not help but drift to the young girl, stealing tentative glimpses of her while she watched and listened to the Elders.

She was about his age, with her hair pulled back behind her head. The first time that she looked over to the boy and their eyes met, he was captivated by them, immersed in them, and suddenly he was back in his dream from several nights prior, the dream that he had shared with the Elder about being lost in the eyes of a young girl.

"We are just ready for a meal," said the Elder Woman, startling the boy from his trance, and the four of them enjoyed a meal together around the small fire.

During the meal, the Elders continued to converse. The boy studied them as they spoke to each other. It was an easy, comfortable discussion, one not between strangers. They spoke of journeys, of knowledge and wisdom, and from all of it, the boy sensed that between them there had been many things seen and done.

But before long, the boy's attention again drifted to the girl, who sat in silence as she ate, listening to the Elders speaking, as the boy was. Eventually, he found the courage to speak to her.

"We travel East on a journey of great importance," said the boy clumsily, the timing of his statement far from ideal, his mouth partially full of food. But such was the way of infatuation.

The girl smiled at his awkwardness and then replied, "As do we. My Elder guides me East on a journey for a meeting with the Mage."

The boy's jaw stopped, mid-chew, in astonishment.

"To live your Destiny Thread and find the Tapestry of Spirit?" he asked.

Taken aback for an instant at the coincidence, the girl finally managed a response.

"Yes," she said, surprised that she and the unfamiliar boy beside her could be on such a similar journey.

They exchanged smiles and were happy to feel somehow connected by shared purposes.

"Do you know how much further the journey is before you find the Mage?" asked the boy.

"No," replied the girl, "but my Elder tells me that as I continue to follow and live my Destiny Thread, I will eventually meet the Mage and return to the Tapestry of Spirit."

The boy truly felt kindred to the girl, and as she looked at him and he again became lost in her eyes there in the dim firelight, he understood why it was in his dream of her that looking into her eyes was as if looking into his own.

"Perhaps we can journey the rest of the way together," suggested the boy, emboldened by the coincidence of their meeting, thinking and hoping that perhaps the girl was along his path for a reason that was a part of his Destiny Thread.

"It is not the way for this journey," came the Elder's gentle reply from across the fire, having overheard the boy's comment to the girl.

"But we both travel East," questioned the boy.

"Each person's journey East is unique," said the Elder Woman, "and while the end of the journey is the same in finding the Mage and returning to the Tapestry of Spirit, its duration and what is encountered along the way is different for each."

The boy sat, disappointed in the answers from the Elders.

"I know that you wish it to be otherwise, but it is the way of this journey," said the Elder, "the journey that I guide you on."

The Elder woman then added, "For even as two people journey the same path, what they see will be different, as what they need to see will be different, and learned from."

The boy remained saddened, as did the girl at the boy's glance toward her, which both Elders sensed.

"Enjoy this crossing of your Destiny Threads, and enjoy this meal and this evening shared," said the Elder, "and if your Destiny Threads are meant to cross again when your journeys East have concluded, then rejoice in that as well."

The boy, while still saddened that they would likely separate in the morning, understood the value of the moments with the girl on that evening by the fire, and his thoughts turned to the happiness of the evening instead of the sorrow that would come with their parting at the rising of the Sun. The boy also trusted in the wisdom of both his Elder and the girl's Elder, and if their wisdom told that their present journeys were to be separate, then he believed it to be truth.

The boy wanted it to be different, but trusted that it was as it was to be. And in thinking of it further, he knew it to be true, as the Elder had said: this journey was his to take alone, with only the Elder as a guide. The boy knew that along this journey he would change, that truths would be made clear, and answers to unspoken questions revealed, and through all of that, the boy would reach its conclusion as anew. And, he thought, after that time, if it were right that his Destiny Thread and the girl's were to cross again, then it would be so.

The four of them spoke and laughed and enjoyed their union until late into the night, then settled around the fire to sleep.

And as the boy lay near the fire as it gently settled into embers, he looked up to the starry sky above and wondered about how dreams and the World existed together. He thought of how, many nights prior, he had dreamt of going to the center of the marketplace, and when he did go two days later, he met the Elder and his journey began. He then thought of how only a few nights prior, he had dreamt of the girl, and now, lying next to the boy, she existed.

The boy wondered if dreams were responsible for creating the World.

Without knowing the answer, he found his thoughts hoping that it was indeed the case, for dreams of beauty could then create a World of beauty, and he drifted off to sleep.

The boy awoke the following morning with the happiness of the previous evening still in his heart. He looked toward the girl who had slept nearby, who was just awakening as well, and they shared a smile.

The Elders had been awake for a short while, and had prepared a morning meal for them all to share before their separate journeys continued. And as they ate, they re-lived stories and wisdom shared from the previous evening. The boy felt true communion with the Elder Woman and the girl, and he kept at bay the sadness that he knew he would feel once they were on their way again alone.

With the meal finished, the Elders exchanged extended goodbyes as the boy awkwardly struggled with how to convey his feelings toward the girl. Finally, he came upon what to say.

"I hope that our Destiny Threads cross again," he said, getting lost in her eyes for possibly the last time.

"It is my hope as well," replied the girl with a soft smile.

And with that, the boy and the Elder resumed their journey toward the East, leaving the camp and the Elder Woman and the girl behind them, the boy looking back twice to find the girl looking after him on both occasions. Soon, the Elder and the boy had drifted down a gradual slope, and the camp behind them was out of sight.

As they walked, the boy grew sad, and selfishness began to grow within him, drawn to the promise of what being with the girl might hold had he decided to travel with her. He questioned his Destiny Thread. How could it be that his dream from a few nights prior had created the girl, only then to leave her behind on that morning? How could it be that his Destiny Thread would lead him away from someone whose eyes reminded him of his, who so clearly he had connected with in such a short time? Surely, that must have been the Tapestry of Spirit making itself known, he thought. Was perhaps his

Destiny Thread to lead him to being lonely and unhappy? With these thoughts in his head, the boy summoned the courage to question the Elder.

"Could it be that my Destiny Thread is meant to make me unhappy?" he asked the Elder. "Surely, it could be possible, couldn't it?"

At the question, the Elder abruptly stopped and turned to the boy, sadness in his eyes at the boy for having such thoughts.

"Your Destiny Thread leads to, and is a part of the Tapestry of Spirit," he said softly. "*The Tapestry of Spirit*," he repeated with a gentle emphasis that stirred profound feelings within the boy.

"It is the Tapestry that unites all other Destiny Threads together. Its wisdom is beyond what you may believe your truth to be at this moment, as your journey East is not yet complete, but you must believe at all times, and in all circumstances, that your woven presence within it is pure and true, one of belonging that need not ever be questioned."

Although the Elder was in no way admonishing him, the boy lowered his head for allowing his own sudden wants to cause him to question such things.

With a gentle hand, the Elder lifted the boy's head.

"I know of what your heart desires," said the Elder sympathetically, "but on this you must have trust in my guidance. The Mage that awaits you where your Destiny Thread joins the Tapestry of Spirit will make the truth in what I have said clear," he said simply, and smiled.

The boy managed an apologetic smile in return, after which they resumed the journey East, the boy again trusting of the Elder and his wisdom.

Later, the boy's thoughts returned to his musings the prior night as he lay beside the fire to sleep, thoughts about how dreams and the World existed together, and if dreams were responsible for creating the World. The boy shared his thoughts with the Elder, who then offered only a simple reply.

"As I said in the marketplace on the day of our meeting," replied the Elder with a smile, "dreams are mystical," and then said no more.

ᔰ 13 ᔰ

It was the middle of the following day when the boy and the
Elder came upon a curious sight outside of a small village. The
village itself was modest and simple, which made the scene on
its outskirts all the more conspicuous.

A large, caged, wooden wagon, drawn by two enormous
horses, had stopped, a small gathering of local villagers
standing in a group nearby. Between the caged wagon and the
gathering of villagers stood a fearsome looking young warrior
with a large, broad, sheathed sword hanging at one hip, a long
knife hanging at the other. He was very tall, tanned and
muscular, and despite his youthful appearance, carried
numerous scars of conflict on various parts of his body.

Next to the young warrior stood a smaller, round, bearded
man, his age between that of the Elder and the boy. With
golden rings on each finger, the finest of linen covering his

entire rotund body, and belts of gold and silver wrapped around his bulging mid-section, he held a fabric umbrella above his head to shield himself and his pale skin from the heat of the mid-day Sun.

The wagon behind him was most ornate, with intricate carvings all along the entirety of its dark wood frame, and from the edges of the bed of the wagon towered a thick set of equally spaced iron bars that rose up to an ornate, dark wood canopy, the combination forming a complete and rather elegant cage. At the back of the wagon, the cage had a small, hinged door of the same thick bars as the rest of the cage, and was secured with an enormous lock.

Suspended from the wooden canopy from inside the cage was draped a dark blue fabric, arcing down in majestic curves, providing shade to a young boy within who sat upon a small, short stool near the bars at the edge of the wagon. The boy, about the age of the boy who traveled with the Elder, wore a robe of similar dark blue fabric, his head shaved clean to the skin.

The Elder and the boy approached the scene and stopped, keeping their distance for the moment.

One of the villagers then stepped to the small, round man and handed him a coin, to which the round man then motioned to the cage, and the villager proceeded toward it. Once there, the young boy within the cage extended his hands through the iron bars and gently took the villager's hands in his.

As the Elder and the boy watched, the boy in the cage and the villager exchanged quiet words, with the boy in the cage doing most of the speaking. The villager, still holding the boy's hands, looked to the round man keeping watch of him, then the fearsome warrior nearby, then back to the boy within the cage.

The villager and the boy in the cage then released hands, the boy withdrawing his within the cage and then clasping them together in a spiritual salutation to the villager, who returned the gesture and then returned to the group.

As the next villager from the group stepped to the round man, paid him a coin, and then proceeded to the side of the cage to speak with the boy within it, the Elder and the boy stepped forward.

"What happens here?" asked the Elder of the round man.

The round man smiled, revealing a broad, dingy smile of crooked teeth.

"I offer time with the boy," he said casually. "He is a Monk who tells of people's Destinies…for a price."

The statement troubled the boy standing beside the Elder, and he was compelled to speak.

"I am in pursuit of my Destiny," said the boy, "but my guide does not profit from me for it."

The round man laughed aloud before replying.

"Well, if you believe that there is wisdom in what the Monk says, which I do not, you will have to accept that it is purely because it is your Destiny to not be profited from."

"So, you profit from the Monk's words, yet you do not believe in them?" asked the boy.

"Correct," said the round man flatly. "But that does not mean that they are not valued by others."

The boy looked to the boy Monk in the cage, then back to the round man, and felt anger within him continuing to grow.

"How is it just that you hold him captive and profit from his wisdom?" the boy asked bluntly.

The round man laughed again and then replied, "It must be my destiny," to which, greatly amused by his own sarcasm toward the boy, he laughed aloud again.

The boy was very angered by the answers of the man that stood before him, which only seemed to provide further amusement and reason for continued condescending laughter from the round man.

When the round man stopped laughing, he spoke again.

"But, many seasons ago, after I claimed ownership of the Monk, I did make a promise to my 'Destiny' and the 'Tapestry' that the Monk speaks of. With the door to the cage locked securely, I threw the key into a large river many, many day's travel from here. I proclaimed to the boy, as well as to this

'Destiny Thread' and mystical 'Tapestry', wherever they may reside, that I would free him if the key ever found its way back to the lock."

The round man then paused and sarcastically shrugged his shoulders, flashing his crooked smile and releasing an amused chuckle.

This angered the boy even more, and he eyed the motionless warrior standing next to the round man. He was truly an imposing figure, and the boy quickly understood why it was that the round man would need such a person with him on his journeys with his captive.

But in an instant, the boy's anger was replaced with a hope, and he quickly removed his pack and searched within it, confusing the round man. A moment later, the boy held out an opened hand to the round man. And in his opened hand rested a large key, the key given to him by the grieving Mother only several nights prior, the key that the Mother's son had found in a river many seasons ago.

Although it had been many seasons since the round man had thrown the key into the river far, far away, he recognized it in an instant. And upon seeing the key in the boy's hand, the pompous expression on the round man's face vanished and all color drained from his face. Even his lips went pale and they began to quiver, and the fabric umbrella lowered and fell to the ground beside him.

The round man remained where he stood, staring first at the key in the boy's outstretched hand, then looking to the boy Monk who sat quietly in the cage observing them, then back to the key in the boy's hand.

From the round man's inaction, the warrior emerged from his silence.

"Although you have always mocked it," the warrior began, speaking to the round man in a low but powerful voice, "it is now time that you honor the Tapestry of Spirit."

The warrior stepped forward, took the key from the boy's hand, and started toward the cage.

The round man's face had now contorted into shame and he fell heavily to his knees, bringing the ringed fingers of both hands up to cover his face as he began to weep. The years of willful greed and unjust captivity at the boy Monk's expense came flooding from him, and the life that he felt he knew would be gone in the next instant.

At the cage, the warrior carefully inserted the key into the large lock, paused to look back to the boy and the Elder, and then turned the key within the lock. The lock on the cage door opened, and the gathered villagers gasped, with some beginning to weep quietly at what had happened before them.

The warrior opened the cage door and held out a large, gentle hand for the Monk to take as he stepped out of the cage and onto the soil of the World. It was a feeling he had not felt for a very, very long time.

The boy Monk proceeded, with the warrior behind him, to where the round man was huddled on the ground, now weeping loudly.

As the Monk approached, the round man looked up to him, his face wet with tears, and he reached up pleading hands toward the Monk.

"Forgive, please forgive," begged the round man hysterically.

The Monk, sympathy in his eyes, remained motionless before the round man on the ground as he continued through his sobs.

"Please...forgive...I beg..." the round man pleaded, as he again hunched over in a heap upon himself, now openly sobbing before the young Monk.

With the eyes of all upon him, the Monk knelt down and placed a gentle hand on the shoulder of his captor.

"Forgiveness is not for me to give to you, but for you to give to yourself," said the Monk softly.

The round man's head lifted as his sobbing subsided slightly at the words, and he looked to the Monk kneeling beside him.

"But I have caged you and profited from you and traveled well over great distances in doing so," he said.

"And in doing so, I have been able to spread the wisdom of the Threads of Destiny and the Tapestry of Spirit," replied the Monk calmly.

For the first time in all the many seasons that they had been in each other's presence, the round man looked into the eyes of the boy Monk and saw him for what he was: a boy. He then looked fearfully to the gathered villagers that now surrounded them, suddenly afraid of their possible wrath now that the Monk was freed.

"Over the seasons," continued the Monk, "I have told those that have paid you to speak with me not to have anger toward you, which they had, but to instead understand that you were one that was not being true to your Destiny Thread, and that I was along to help you to realize it."

It was then that the round man realized that over the seasons, it had been the young boy Monk that had taken care of him, not the round man of him. And the boy, standing next to the Elder, saw that in a way, the boy Monk in the cage was the one who had been guiding the round man all along, patiently waiting for what happened on that day.

The round man turned to the warrior, who had been silent.

"And you...you could have easily killed me and eventually found a way to free the Monk," said the round man.

"To kill a man leaves but a dead man, but to educate a man leaves a teacher," said the warrior flatly.

"Besides, it was not my Destiny Thread to do so," added the warrior, looking to the boy Monk, then back to the round man on the ground.

"For while you slept each night, gorged on the finest meats that your profits could buy, the Monk and I had many conversations about Threads of Destiny and the Tapestry of Spirit," said the warrior. "Our Destiny Threads crossed many seasons ago for a purpose, and now that purpose is clear to you. As I protected him, I protected you, both the Monk and I waiting until the arrival of this day."

The round man looked confused, but the Monk helped him to understand.

"Our Destiny Threads crossed so that you could, one day, more clearly see yours," said the boy Monk. "A seed planted at dusk does not yield a tree by dawn."

The last statement caught the boy as he stood next to the Elder, as it was what the Sage under the tree had said only evenings before.

The Monk continued. "And now, other Destiny Threads have led to ours and have made us all equals in your eyes and revealed to you the Tapestry of Spirit."

The round man's eyes welled again with tears, not from shame, but rather from gratitude, and he stood, and in standing, his very posture changed: from the stooped, sullen, shamed figure rose a straight, upright form, as if he himself had been freed from his own cage.

"I have ignored and mocked these things over these many seasons," said the round man softly, "but now that I see them clearly, I shall be true in following them, on this I give my word. My travels from this day forward will be to share of the wealth that I possess, and of this wisdom that you have bestowed upon me."

The Monk and the warrior looked at each other and smiled.

"And we shall continue to travel with you," the Monk said, overwhelming the round man again to tears at the forgiving Nature of the boy Monk.

And with that, the round man began to return the payment to the villagers who had paid to speak with the Monk that day.

The Monk turned to the Elder and the boy. "The Tapestry of Spirit is truly present today," he said, smiling.

"We travel East," said the boy, "and my guide journeys with me, as I am in search of my own Destiny Thread and the Tapestry of Spirit."

The boy Monk smiled broadly and said, "Then good fortune is mine today, for I am from the East, but it has been many seasons since being taken and held in the cage. I would like to inform those from where I come that I am well and living my Destiny Thread, but that I now follow it elsewhere.

May I ask for you to go to the place that I am from and share this?" he asked politely.

"Certainly," said the boy, which pleased the Monk.

"I am very grateful for this," said the young Monk. "A day's travel East from here lies a small city next to the Sea, and across that Sea on the other side, there is another, much larger city. That is where I am from. On every eve of a new moon, there is a great gathering in a circular stone amphitheatre at the city center, in which Holy leaders gather. It is known as the Circle of Beliefs. At that gathering, you will see a group that is from the East, with the speaker of that group being a wise Wholy Woman. It is to her that I wish for you to impart this knowledge about my condition."

The boy nodded in understanding.

"My name is Javell," said the Monk, to which the Elder and the boy could only silently look to each other.

"We will pass along our knowledge of you," said the boy.

The Monk smiled, bringing his clasped hands to his heart and gesturing.

"I wish you safe travels to the East, and to the Tapestry of Spirit," he said.

The Elder and the boy returned the gesture, bid farewell to the round man, the warrior, and the villagers, and then continued on, passing through the small village on their journey toward the East, toward the Sea that the Monk said lay before them.

And as they journeyed the rest of that day, the boy reflected on how prevalent the items of which he sought seemed to be. It seemed that now, all around him, was mention of Destiny Threads, the Tapestry of Spirit, and the Mage, yet up until only a few days prior to when he had met the Elder in the marketplace, he had never in his life heard of such things.

Then it occurred to the boy why, as it was as the Sage had said, that those that seek are often bound by what they are taught and not of what they know, and the simple reason as to why the boy had never before heard mention of these things that he sought was clear: he had never before looked.

By nightfall, the Elder and the boy had made camp in flatlands, and gazing into the flames of their small fire, the boy spoke of the Sea crossing that lay ahead of them.

"Have you journeyed on the Seas?" asked the boy of the Elder.

"Yes, I have journeyed on many Seas," came the reply.

"What is it like?" asked the boy, his eyes having never seen a vast body of water, much less been upon one.

The Elder thought for a moment before replying.

"It is to be a part of this, and of that, both at the same time," he said, which puzzled the boy. But the boy did not feel the need to ask further questions, as he believed that soon enough he would understand what it was that the Elder meant.

14

The following morning, the boy and the Elder consumed the last of their provisions and resumed the journey with empty packs. And again, the boy's thoughts drifted, but only for an instant, to how they would be sustained. But as quickly as the concern arrived, the boy dismissed it, trusting that the journey would somehow sustain them when needed, as it had up to that point.

By mid-day they crested a small ridge, beyond which and in the distance lay a small port city, with a vast Sea beyond it.

The sight of the sprawling body of water, even from the distance, was as awe-inspiring to the boy as he had imagined, sparking deep intrigue within him. The Sea stretched to the horizon and beyond, and he could only wonder where, in all of its vastness, the large port city that they sought on the other side might lie.

By the middle of the afternoon, they had entered the outskirts of the small city by the edge of the Sea, and before long, they had traversed the sleepy, narrow streets and found themselves approaching the docks near the water.

As they neared the docks, they walked along a row of small cottages that looked out to the docks and beyond to the Sea. In front of one such cottage sat a man, roughly twice the boy's age. The man's appearance shocked the boy, for he was emaciated, almost skeletal, his skin a tired hue of light grey. The man labored greatly even to breathe, so much so that his entire torso lifted and fell with each breath, and it struck the boy that the man's age and his condition did not seem to be in harmony. The man's gaze was on the Sea, a weary and melancholy gaze that failed to shift even as the boy and the Elder began to pass by in front of him on their way to the docks.

But something about the man moved the boy to stop, something more than the man's gaze locked on the Sea. Perhaps it was the sadness that he sensed within him. Or perhaps it was because, from the man's age, he was about the age that his own Father would have been.

At the boy stopping just beyond the front of the man's cottage, the Elder stopped. The boy took a few steps toward the man and offered a greeting, at which the man turned his weary head, closely eyeing both he and the Elder, especially the boy, and as he eyed the boy, the boy studied the man's face. His broad nose and square jaw, together with what was left of what surely was once a strong and fit body, would have made the man an imposing figure in seasons past, the boy thought.

The man's gaze remained on the boy's face, studying it, looking for something within it. The boy remained silent as the man studied him, and after a moment, the man's attention finally reached some sad, silent conclusion about the boy.

"Forgive me," said the man with a labored breath, "it was not my intention to be unfriendly."

The boy and the Elder smiled to put the man at ease.

"Forgive me," replied the boy, "for it was not my intention to be overly curious. But I could not help but wonder what the Sea might offer that could hold your gaze in such a way."

The man looked sadly to his clasped hands in his lap.

"It is not the Sea itself, but what lies beyond," he began, his words sounding through his wheezing. "My life has seen many wasted seasons, and my only redemption lies on the other side of the water."

"Not all are meant to walk in the light of their truth in every moment," offered the Elder. "It is the moments that we travel off the path and into darkness that can be the most illuminating."

The man smiled in appreciation of the Elder's kindness.

"Long ago," continued the man, laboring to breathe, "in the city to the East on the other side of the Sea, I left someone dear to me. I left not because of lack of love, but out of love, as my ways would have surely brought peril, an undeserved and unjust peril, to those around me. And those perils would have brought down consequences upon the innocent that I could not have borne."

The man looked from his lap and up to the boy.

"It was my young son," said the man, a great sadness now clearly upon his features as he began to relay the story between the heaves of his chest.

"There was much love for him in my heart, but because I followed darkened paths in the World, I feared someday that those paths would lead to him. And so, one night, when the moon was new, and before my son would have any memory of me, I left the place that I called my home, hopeful that those around him would rear him to a good man, unlike his Father."

The man's history affected the boy, as he reflected on how the events in this man's past were similar to events in his own life when he was a young boy, and how his own Father had gone before the boy had any memories of him.

As he became emotional, the man began to cough, a deep, subdued, rumbling cough that remained within his chest, pushing hardly anything from it. In a moment, he had overcome it and continued.

"I spent all the seasons from that one to this on the Seas of the World to the West, in a fog that would never lift, hoping that the waves of the water would wash the pain and disappointment in myself from my heart," said the man somberly. "And it came to be that this season would be the one when the fog lifted, as I finally had found the way to travel the darkened paths no more. But upon returning from the Seas of the West, and arriving at this small port city, I contracted the sickness that now grows within my chest.

The man again began to cough as before, again concerning the boy and the Elder, but after a moment it had passed.

"I attempted the final crossing of the Sea to the East, to return to the innocence that I had abandoned so many seasons ago, but my failing body could not endure the motion of the waves and how it strained the breath left within me, and I was forced to return here," said the man, who then looked to the boy before continuing.

"So it is now, in the final season of my life, with my small boat tied to the dock, waiting for me to again attempt a journey that I would never complete, that I seek only one thing: for words to fall upon my son's ears, words that say nothing more than I loved him then as I love him now."

And again, the man gasped and began to cough the weak, sickly, rumbling cough that wracked his body from the sickness in his chest for which there was no remedy.

When the coughing subsided, the man again looked out to the vastness of the Sea, his gaze hoping somehow to reach the other side.

"But with each day, stranded as I am here, my heart indulges a hope, a fool's dream that my son might be in search of me," said the man. "And so here I sit, everyday, and watch for a boat to approach from the horizon that may carry him to me."

The regretful Father looked again to his hands in sad acceptance. "But I know this is not likely, for my remaining days are short, and if not for the warmth of the Sun on this frail body, it would surely go cold and turn to dust."

The boy was very moved by the sorrow in the man, and he wondered what he himself would say to the man if he were his Father. But foremost in the boy was the urge to comfort him in some way, and he knew that what he would say next would do so.

"We travel East, across the Sea, to the port city on the other side," said the boy, "in search of a great stone amphitheater and the Circle of Beliefs within it. All we seek for this journey is a boat."

The man's head lifted and he looked with hopeful eyes to the boy. The boy looked to the Elder for agreement on what the boy himself would say next, and with a nod and a smile from the Elder, the boy continued.

"We shall find your son on the other side and deliver your message," said the boy, to which tears filled the eyes of the man, and the boy was moved by the emotion that his words had brought to him.

The boy did not know how he and the Elder would come to find the man's son in the large city, but he somehow believed in his heart that they would, and that was all that was needed for the boy to proclaim what he did. It was as if the mere act of saying the words made them a truth waiting to be realized.

The man eventually composed himself to speak.

"Then with each rising of the Sun that remains for me," began the man, his voice broken, "I shall look across the water with the belief that somehow my final message will soon be heard."

And with that, the man struggled and then rose, with the help of the boy and the Elder, and led them inside his small cottage and fed them a meal of bread and fish. As they ate, and despite his many seasons at Sea, the man only spoke of memories of his infant son, happy memories that seemed to cheer him. And it was having the boy and the Elder to share of the memories that was special to the man, for in his traveled life, he had not come to keep those around him that cared.

Giving the man hope that his final wish would be realized pleased the boy very much, and he reflected again on his own youth and chose to believe that his own Father had left for reasons such as the man's, that he somehow had left out of love for him.

After eating, the man filled the empty packs of the boy and the Elder, the boy's trust in the journey sustaining them evident before his eyes yet again. Along with the provisions, the man gave the boy a small root that he said would be useful during the crossing. The three of them stepped from the cottage and back to where the man had been sitting.

"My boat is just there," said the man, pointing to a small, lone, two-oared skiff in the water near the docks. "Since my son could not yet walk when I left him so many seasons ago, all that I can tell you of him is his name, which graces the back of my boat."

The man again expressed his great thanks to them, holding his cupped hands to his heart, and with that, the Elder and the boy returned the gesture and started down the docks for the boat.

Once they had reached the small boat, the Elder stepped in first and sat, laying first his pack and then the boy's on the bottom of the boat. He then helped the unsteady and nervous boy into the craft. The experience was very new to the boy, and although he could not swim, he found that his excitement for the crossing of the water with a message such as the one they carried was stronger than his fear of the water.

With the boy seated, the Elder untied the boat from the dock, took the two oars that rested inside the boat and placed them into their cradles, then gently pushed the boat away from the dock. They turned back to see the man sitting again in front of his cottage. He raised a thin arm in farewell, to which the Elder and the boy waved back, and then the Elder took the oars in hand and began to row them out into the calm waters of the small bay, beyond which lay the open Sea.

In the few seasons of the boy's young life, he had never seen a body of water such as this: not a pond, nor a lake, and certainly not something as vast as a Sea. And because of this, the boy had never traveled by boat before, never glided upon the surface of water. So as the Elder rowed the small boat across the calm bay, the boy was deeply moved by the experience. As they entered the depths of the bay, the boy reached a hand over the side and into the warm, darkening water. It was a profound experience for him, to feel so connected to something so vast.

Before long, they had left the calm waters of the small bay and had entered into the gentle, rhythmic waves of the Sea. As the boat began to rock gently, the boy had his first experience of the power of the open waters. With each wave that gently moved the boat, the boy wondered from where it had come, what distant force had created it, to have likely traveled very, very far to so gently lap at the side of their small boat.

The Elder interrupted his thoughts with instructions that the boy chew some of the root that the dying Father had placed into his pack, a root that would prevent the wave sickness during the three days that it would take for the crossing. The boy complied, and as he chewed on the bitter root, his mind drifted back to the motion of the water, and the rhythm of the gentle waves. And in his thoughts, the boy found himself thinking of the man whose message they carried, and he thought about the passage of time. He looked at the Elder as he rowed, trying for the first time along the journey to estimate his age. The Elder noticed the boy studying him, and smiled.

"What question do you wish to ask of me?" asked the Elder.

The boy grinned and asked, "What is your age?"

The Elder smiled and then replied, "I am many ages, all at once," he said. "From each day since my beginning, to this moment. I am not a point on my Destiny Thread, but rather the collection of all points along its path to now."

"Do you feel that any of the days of your past have escaped you, like the owner of this boat?" asked the boy.

"Spending each day in truth to your Destiny Thread can never result in lost days," answered the Elder. "It is only when we choose not to follow that truth that we feel the days of the past were misspent."

The boy thought back on the days of his relatively short life and reflected on the words of the Elder. He remembered how, when he was young, every day seemed anew, full of hope and adventure and possibility, and it seemed to the boy that there had been no days ever lost or misspent during his youth.

But since the passing of his Mother, and the changes in his life that followed when he was forced as a boy into the World of men, his days seemed shallow and pale, merely echoes of what they could hold. It was the repetition of so many empty days over the past seasons since her passing that had finally compelled the boy to dream as he did, which eventually led him to the Elder.

"But even with a belief that days or seasons have been misspent," said the Elder, "it is never beyond one's reach to extend a hand across lost distance and time, as you are helping the owner of this boat to do."

The boy smiled, and hoped that upon their arrival at the land across the Sea, they would somehow find the son of the man whose message they carried.

"It seems that we now carry two messages," remarked the boy, one of the boy Monk that they had freed from the cage with the grieving Mother's key, and one from the dying Father on the docks seeking a final message be delivered to his lost son.

"We are all messengers," replied the Elder, "with each message a reminder of the Tapestry of Spirit, for the messages we carry to strangers bind us together, as the Tapestry of Spirit does."

The boy thought on this for a moment before replying.

"Are there messages for us that are carried by others?"

The Elder smiled and then answered, "Every word of meaning shared between strangers is a message."

The boy then saw, in his life, how words spoken between strangers had the ability to connect them, both in good ways and bad, and while the good ways drew them together, the bad ways pushed them apart. And in thinking about feeling distant from those with whom bad words were shared, he thought back to the wisdom of the Sage when he spoke of the Tapestry of Spirit unraveling when those in the World of men did not live their Destiny Thread and honor the single strand at its core. He again wondered what the strand was, at the core of all Destiny Threads and therefore the Tapestry of Spirit, and looked forward to learning what it was from the Mage, as the Sage had said he would.

❧ 15 ❧

As the Sun rose to its peak in the sky overhead, the Elder paused his methodical rowing, and he and the boy enjoyed a meal from the provisions that the man had given them. And as they ate, several porpoise leapt from the water nearby, then plunged back down, wetting the boy and the Elder.

The boy was frightened at the appearance of the animals of the Sea, especially being so close to the small boat, but the Elder quickly assured him that they meant no harm to them.

"They journey as we do," said the Elder, "only their journey is below the water while ours is above."

Calmed, the boy cautiously looked over the side of the boat and into the dark water, and again lowered his hand into its warmth as he had done while they were in the bay. He wondered about how deep the Seas were, and how much water and life there must be within them. He thought about what a divide there seemed to be between the World of water and the World of air. Yet, there in the boat, in and on the water as he was, the boy connected the two incredibly vast states of things, air and water, and felt a moving sense of presence at being a part of both at the same time, with one hand in water and one in air. Being on the Sea was just as the Elder had said it would be earlier that day: 'It is to be a part of this, and of that, both at the same time.'

After they ate, the Elder resumed rowing East, and throughout the rest of the day, he and the boy were treated to several more displays of life in the Sea as it emerged to greet those that journeyed upon the water. And the boy came to view the Sea, and all that lived within it, as in balance in its Nature, just as the great tree was that the Sage lived beneath. And as the great tree was a testament to the Tapestry of Spirit lived, the Sea was as well.

The Elder rowed until the setting of the Sun behind them, then lifted the oars and placed them inside the boat. He and the boy shared an evening meal, and then lay in the bottom of the boat as the sky darkened and the stars began to appear. After a while, the crescent of a nearly new moon rose above them, and not long after that, the gentle rocking of the boat and the fatigue of the day's journey had nudged them into sleep.

They awoke the following morning as the Sun began to lighten the sky in the East ahead of them. The Elder, in looking to the West, saw dark clouds gathered on the horizon.

"It will storm today," said the Elder calmly, directing the boy's attention to the menacing clouds behind them. Despite their distance from them in only the pre-dawn light, they appeared ominous to the boy, and concern stirred within him of what they might bring their way.

After a morning meal, the Elder placed the oars in their cradles and began methodically rowing toward the rising Sun at his back, and throughout the morning, the boy turned frequently to seek the position of the dark clouds behind them to the West, each time finding them closer than they had been before.

By mid-day, the clouds were upon them. Now a wide, black mass, so black that they seemed to lack any definition, they obscured the Sun above and loomed down upon them in the boat.

As the breeze churned to a wind and the Sea became great, rolling waves, fear filled the boy at their situation: there, in a small boat in the middle of the heaving Sea, with no land in sight and the port city ahead of them somewhere still another day away, the boy's thoughts were suddenly on his mortality.

"Secure the packs beneath your bench," shouted the Elder over the wind, which snapped the boy from his fearful concerns. And as the boy did as he was told, the Elder began to forcefully pull on the oars of the boat in order to position it amidst the growing waves.

Soon, the small boat was rocking violently, as larger and larger waves appeared and the wind pushed them this way and that, the boy clinging to the sides of the boat and the Elder straining at the oars to maintain the positioning of the boat. And it was then that the driving rains began, as the worst of the storm set upon them.

As the mighty waves and wind and rain battered them, the small boat would descend into great troughs with towering walls of dark water all around. And in the depths of the troughs, the boy felt as if at the bottom of a deep, dark, inescapable pit, where no hope and no happiness and no light existed, only darkness and despair, certain that at any moment, the giant waves that surrounded them would drop down and crush the small boat, drowning them both.

But from the lowest depths of the troughs, the boat would then rise up the mighty walls of water, up to finally crest at the tops of giant swells that accompanied the troughs, giving the boy visibility to the rest of the entire Sea around him, filling him with hope and promise and courage that they would not only survive the storm, but that they would reach the safe, distant shores of the land to the East.

But from the highest heights of the swells, the boat would then again descend into the lowest depths of the troughs, the pattern repeating itself again and again, becoming a blurred thread of conflicting emotions within the boy, all the while the Elder working feverishly to steer the boat among the threatening waves.

This repetition continued on relentlessly, the boy losing all thought of how long the storm had raged. At one of the crests, a rogue wave struck the side of the boat with such force that the boat tipped up on one side, tearing both the oars from the Elder's grip and nearly launching him into the water, his legs ending up in the Sea while his torso remained in the boat.

The boy was not so lucky, having been flung out into the black water some distance from the boat. And as he thrashed and gasped and coughed in the heaving Sea with the rain and wind beating down upon him, forcing him under the surface of the water time and again, things began to go dim. But as he felt his entire body begin its last descent beneath the waves, a strong hand grasped his upper arm, and as he was pulled from the water, he saw that he was somehow next to the boat with the Elder leaning over its side above him.

With an awkward yank, the Elder pulled the retching boy up from the water and over the side of the boat, the two of them landing in a heap in its bottom. Once safely back in, the terrified boy desperately grasped both sides of the boat, as did the Elder. But the boy noticed then that something was gone from the boat. He looked out to where he had been thrown into the Sea, and through the blinding rains and out across the heaving waters, he caught a final glimpse of the oars as the rolling waves pulled them out of sight.

While the repetition of the troughs and swells would continue unmercifully in the boat, the repetition of alternating emotions that accompanied them in the boy's mind had ended. Gone were the light and hope and promise of reaching the land to the East, the boat now freely being tossed about with the Elder having no way to guide it, and a pervasive, dark certainty settled into the boy that he would meet his end there in the storm that day.

This certainty then slowly turned to an acceptance by the boy of his mortality, but in what he believed to be his final moments, the boy thought not of the doom that awaited him, but instead of the hope that he had felt while on his journey with the Elder. He thought of all that he had seen and done along the quest, including the meeting of the young girl who journeyed East as he did, and how by all of it, even if over only a handful of days up to then, the boy felt alive and true again in some way.

Had he never questioned his path over the previous several seasons, the boy thought, he would never have had his dream which led to the meeting of the Elder, and from that, the grand undertaking that he was on. And he realized that, even if short, he would choose a life lived in pursuit of his truth, meaning, and his Destiny Thread, over a longer life whose final day could bring nothing of note from its length to comfort him.

And in his mind, with that perspective, he felt a calm, despite the calamity that continued to rage around them. He lay down in the bottom of the heaving boat and simply closed his eyes.

❧ 16 ❧

With a dawn sky just beginning to lighten, something caused the sleeping boy in the bottom of the boat to stir. After a moment, it happened again, this time waking the boy, and as he opened his eyes to see a clear sky above him, he realized that somehow, he and the Elder had survived the storm.

Now, no wind howled, no rain fell, and the Sea was so calm that the boy could not perceive the boat rocking at all. And as he lay there in shallow water in the bottom of the boat, water that had collected during the storm, with the Elder sleeping beside him, he heard something against the side of the boat next to him. It was the sound that had caused him to stir and wake, and as the boy sat up, with a calm, flat Sea surrounding them for as far as the eye could see, he looked over the side of the boat to find the two oars floating in the water, gently rubbing against the boat.

It was at that moment, despite the absolute isolation of his situation there in the middle of the calm Sea, that the boy felt his presence as a part of something so vast as to be nearly inconceivable. And it was this feeling within the boy that deeply affected his essence, so much so that his only belief was that he was experiencing the Tapestry of Spirit itself.

There, in such a place of simplicity, the boy had clarity like he had never known before.

And while he sat there in the boat, many things moved through his mind. He thought about the Elder, and how he appreciated him so for his guidance during the journey, and especially for his rescue during the storm. He thought of the oars returning, to allow the boy's journey to continue with the important messages that were carried. And he thought of the seasons ahead of him, of the hope that he held for them, and what events they would hold for him.

The boy reached over the side of the boat and into the water, grasped the oars, and lifted them each up and over the side, returning them to their rightful place in their cradles on each side of the boat. As he did this, the Elder woke and sat up. The boy expected a surprised reaction from the Elder, but there was none. He seemed to merely acknowledge what had happened, that the oars had returned to them so that the boy's journey could continue. And it was to the boy yet again that the journey would provide them what was needed for him to reach it's conclusion, and that Nature had been at work to keep things in balance.

The boy then retrieved the wet packs from under the bench and he and the Elder ate a meal in silence before the Elder continued to row East toward the rising Sun.

For the rest of the morning, the boy was in profound thought and said nothing as the Elder rowed. On occasion, he would look to the Elder and smile, a simple smile in recognition of things, and then return his gaze to the calm Seas that surrounded them.

The boy thought of what were called coincidences, things that happened that seemed to be somehow aligned perfectly to other things, and how they were usually so quickly defined as luck or favorable chance, yet never described as possibly being a part of something else, something of which all were connected.

Any doubt that may have remained in the boy's heart and mind as to the existence of the Tapestry of Spirit, remained no more.

After a while, the boy spoke of his feelings during the storm.

"I felt as a pendulum in the storm," he started, "at one moment feeling the despair and fear of the depths of the waves, then swinging into the next moment to the hope and triumph of their peaks."

"Which did you prefer?" asked the Elder.

"The peaks, of course," replied the boy.

"But without the depths of the troughs, the heights of the swells would have less meaning," said the Elder. "It is not a flaw in Nature that both exist, as one is given meaning by the other, and because of that, both are equally important. The flaw is of man in deeming one as desirable and the other not, for to do so is to deny that they both are needed in the Nature of things."

"But how is it desirable to feel despair and fear?" questioned the boy.

"To focus only on the feelings that they bring is to not recognize the true lessons within them," replied the Elder. "The Sea from last evening is a mirror to life and one's Destiny Thread. The troughs and swells exist together, as they are of the same creation. Each reveals the other, and to separate them is to tear at the very balance of Nature."

The boy reflected on the duality that the Elder described, and realized the wisdom in what he had said. For when fear and despair were at their greatest within the boy during the storm—with the oars lost, waves crashing all around, and his death believed to be near—from this came the boy's reasons for his journey: to seek the answers to his unspoken questions, and to realize the meaning in his life that they would bring.

And it was as if reflection on his greatest fear yielded the reflection on his greatest gratitude, and it was this gratitude that enabled the boy to see that morning's light.

"It is difficult to remember those things while they are being felt," said the boy, thinking to how lacking of hope he felt during the storm.

"To feel them in balance is to know that while feeling one, there exists its other," said the Elder. "In times of plenty, remain humble in recognition of times of need, and in times of need, remain hopeful in recognition of times of plenty. While one looks into a mirror, its mate is reflected."

And with that statement by the Elder, with reference to a mirror and a mate, the boy again thought back on the meeting of the young girl that also journeyed East. He reflected on the dream that he had had of seeing her in the misty frame, and how, upon actually meeting her a few days later, he had felt that they were one and the same.

Around mid-morning, as the Elder continued his rowing toward the East, the boy glimpsed land in the distance ahead of them, what appeared to be the edge of a sprawling city, and he was filled with relief and excitement.

Beyond the thoughts of safety that the land ahead of them offered, and beyond the thought that his journey to find his Destiny Thread, meet the Mage, and return to the Tapestry of

Spirit would continue, the boy then thought of the boy Monk's message that they carried, and then that of the dying Father.

Even with the city on the shore still some distance away from them, it sprawled across the edge of the water, and the boy began to feel discouraged at how they would ever find the man's son in such a vast place.

It was the emergence of doubtful thoughts within the boy, thoughts that darkened him with the difficulty of the task that lie ahead, that caused him to weigh them in his mind, and in weighing them, he concluded that there was no reason to have such thoughts, for they shrouded his search for the man's son in failure before it had even begun.

And so, with firm resolve, he decided to simply not allow the doubts to reside within his thoughts, and that he would not slip back into the World of men, where it was commonplace to be skeptical of things that should be hopeful. Instead, the boy decided that he would just believe—believe that with such a true purpose as to find a lost son to deliver his dying Father's final message, anything was possible.

ᔰ 17 ᕔ

By mid-day, the boy and the Elder had reached the calmer waters of the large bay near the port city, and found themselves among a variety of much larger boats heading to and from the city, coming and going from a variety of directions.

After navigating the busy waterways, the Elder saw a place to dock the boat, and upon reaching it, the boy began to retrieve their packs from under his bench.

"Shift provisions from one pack to the other, so that one pack is full," directed the Elder, as he stepped from the boat and onto the dock.

The boy did not understand why he was asked to do this, but complied nonetheless, moving most of the contents from one pack to the other, leaving one pack full, the other containing only a half-full water skin and a small amount of food.

"Leave the full pack in the boat," added the Elder.

This confused the boy even more, but he did as he was told and without question, placing the full pack beneath his bench in the boat.

The Elder helped the boy up out of the boat and onto the dock, the Elder taking the nearly-empty pack from the boy and placing it upon his back.

And as they stepped away from the boat tied there at the docks, they looked back to the boat's stern for the clue to whom they sought, and once seen, it brought the boy's mind back to the love that the Father across the water felt for his son. And again, the boy found himself believing that his own Father had felt the same love for him so many seasons prior.

With this knowledge in mind—the name of whom they sought—the Elder and the boy started toward where the docks met the city, the place where they would begin their search for the son whose Father's message they carried.

As the boy looked from the North to the South, across the sprawling edge of the city, he was amazed at how large and bustling it all was, and the sheer number of people that the boy saw along its edge made him wonder how many people there were at its heart beyond.

As the boy and the Elder traversed the maze of docks that bordered the city, they merged into streams of people. Sailors, boat workers, passengers arriving on large boats, and fishermen, all of them moving together down the docks and toward the city, and soon, they found themselves approaching the end of the docks and the edge of the city.

As they stepped from the docks, they noticed a young man just older than the boy standing to the side of the stream of people that passed by. And as the stream of arriving people moved past him, the young man intently and hurriedly studied each of their faces, but said not a word to any of them. The young man looked somehow familiar to the boy, even from the distance, and it was only when they neared the young man that the reason why became clear to the boy, who stopped, as did the Elder.

In the young man, the boy recognized a broad nose and a square jaw, similar to those of the dying man across the Sea.

The boy could only stand and stare at the young man, his thoughts on the power of belief earlier in the day returning to him.

It was then that the young man noticed the boy staring at him, and he stared back without reason, unsure of the reason for the boy's interest in him.

"Greetings," said the Elder to the young man, to which he smiled in reply.

The Elder's voice returned the boy from his thoughts, enough for him to speak next.

"We travel in search of the Circle of Beliefs at the center of this city," said the boy, "to provide a message to a great and wise Wholy Woman from a boy Monk lost long ago."

The man nodded and replied, "Yes, the Circle of Beliefs is not far from here," pointing to the center of the city behind him. "It is held in the great stone amphitheatre in the heart of the city, and you will be able to find it easily. Your timing is good, as there is a new moon tonight, and so there will be a gathering," he said before returning his gaze back to the crowded docks and to the Sea beyond.

The boy recognized the young man's voice, for it was as that of the dying man on the other side of the Sea in its tone, its depth, even its pace, and the boy smiled to himself at how the path, as it always had during the journey, was being made clear. That the moment earlier in the day spent in doubt of finding the man that now stood before them had been but a moment wasted, and the decision by the boy to banish the doubt from his mind may have indeed been what led to this meeting. And the boy then wondered: does the power of his thought create the World?

Noting the young man's gaze back to the Sea, the boy asked, "Do you seek someone?"

The young man looked back to the boy and smiled, recognizing that his attention had drifted elsewhere, and then replied.

"Yes," said the young man thoughtfully, "someone from many, many seasons ago. One who had ventured West after living here in this city for a time."

"And why do you seek such a person?" asked the boy, hoping that the young man's answer would further confirm his identity.

The young man became lost in reflection for a moment, as if recounting lost days and seasons in his life, before he replied.

"To show to his eyes that there is nothing within me but understanding and love."

The boy was moved at what lie in the young man's heart. He marveled at what existed there. The young man was quiet for a moment more before he spoke again.

"I always believed that one day he would return," he said, "although I would not know him if he stood before me, as I have no memories of him."

The young man looked again out to the Sea as he continued.

"And so, ever since I was a small boy, I would wait here at the docks each day for the arrival of a man that I had never known. But despite coming here with a heart of hope every day for many, many seasons, it is only lately that I have begun to feel that his return is less and less likely."

The boy believed that the young man was in fact feeling the despair that had settled into his dying Father across the Sea, that although separated by the water and the lost seasons, their Destiny Threads were still connected through the Tapestry of Spirit, and the boy was now connected to them both by the message that he carried between them.

It was the boy who would speak next.

"In addition to seeking the Circle of Beliefs, we are also in search of a young man, the son of a Father who traveled West from here many, many seasons ago, and who now seeks only to deliver a final message to his son."

The young man's eyes widened and his face softened at the words of the boy.

"We carry word from your Father," continued the boy to the young man. "And although his heart wishes him to be here with you now, his body fails him, and it will not be many more days before his final moments."

Tears came to the lost Son's eyes, and the boy saw two emotions mixed upon his face: sadness that his Father's days were quickly coming to an end, yet gratefulness for his Father's desire to return to him before his end of days.

The young man composed himself enough to speak again, asking of the boy, "And what word do you carry on his behalf?"

"That in all the seasons past, since his departure from this place," began the boy, "there was never a lack of love in his heart for you."

The tears in the lost Son's eyes found their way down along his cheeks.

"If only I could ease his passing," he said softly.

The boy was greatly moved by the young man's wish, and it was then that the boy felt something stir within him. The feeling in him was the same feeling that he had had in the boat on that calm morning following the storm. It was the same feeling that he had had in the Sage's presence so many days before. It was a feeling stirred by what was happening before him, that despite many empty seasons passing between the dying Father on the other side of the Sea and his lost Son standing before them, there was only love between them, even still. It was as if, despite the paths that they had followed, they were still connected, still woven together, their Destiny Threads still part of the one Tapestry of Spirit.

The Elder placed a comforting hand on the shoulder of the young man, to which the young man's eyes turned to meet the Elder's.

"There are supplies in a small boat, your Father's boat, that awaits you," said the Elder, to which the young man's eyes filled with hope. "The Sea will be calm for three days, and the winds will favor you," added the Elder.

"What boat?" asked the young man, excitedly scanning the many boats that were tied up along the docks. "Can you show me?"

"It can be found easily among the small boats docked just there," replied the Elder, pointing to the area of the docks where they had left the boat, "for your Father loves you so that his boat bears your name."

"Javell."

The emotion that now left the young man was that from many lost seasons and much empty distance, rendering him without speech.

"Your Father can be found on the other side," continued the Elder, "in front of a cottage near the docks. And although you have never met him, you will know him, for his features are as yours, as is his voice. He waits close to the Sea every day, as you have done here, looking out across its expanse to the East, his only hope that a boat would somehow appear on the horizon carrying you to him."

The Elder paused before making a final statement to the young man.

"And if there is truth in anything in the World, there is truth in this: you will be at your Father's side in his final moments."

And with that, the lost Son, still without words, could only embrace the Elder and the boy, his gaze remaining in the boy's eyes in a final expression of gratitude for the message that he had brought to him from across the Sea.

The young man turned and proceeded hastily onto the docks and toward the boat that awaited him. The Elder and the boy watched after him until he had reached the boat, pausing for a moment at its stern, bringing a hand to his mouth in emotion, and then turning to wave farewell to the boy and the Elder, who waved back.

The boy and the Elder turned to continue East into the heart of the city, and they knew that nightfall would find the young man far out to Sea and on his way to fulfill a final wish.

❧ 18 ❧

As the Elder and the boy journeyed through the large, sprawling port city toward its heart, in search of the large stone amphitheatre and the Circle of Beliefs where the boy Monk in the cage had said the Wholy Woman could be found, the boy was amazed at what he saw.

There were merchants, travelers, shoppers, horses with riders, horses pulling large wagons and carts, mules and donkeys hauling supplies, and men, women, and children of all sorts, all in various garb and from various places across World. It was the largest collection of people the boy had ever been among, and the most diverse. Exotic scents filled the air from foods, perfumes, and spices, all of which were new to the boy. His ears heard words familiar, and others that were not, as they were from distant lands and peoples, foreign tribes and clans. Yet for the great number of people in such proximity to each other, the boy saw singularity and disconnectedness between them.

And as the Elder and the boy moved along with the flow of people, an unexpected thought occurred to the boy; that there existed a Fabric of People.

During his journey with the Elder, the boy held a notion that continually persisted: that everyone could be someone to someone.

Looking at the people that surrounded him, the boy believed that the old man that sat at the edge of the market could be his grandfather. Next to him, the small children running in the streets could one day be his children. The girl his age passing by, carrying a bundle of twigs for making baskets, could be his sister. And yes, even the man and woman walking along the edge of the roadway could be his parents.

But as obvious as the Fabric of People was to the boy, it seemed unrecognized by those around him as they rushed about, bumping and jostling between each other without regard, almost as if in denial of each other's very existence and presence.

The boy wondered if the Fabric of People and the Tapestry of Spirit were somehow related. He mused that the masses living among each other, without connection to each other, were a Fabric of People. Yet the same masses living among each other, with connection to each other, were a Tapestry of Spirit.

As the boy and the Elder ventured deeper into the heart of the vast city, they came upon the sight of an old beggar woman sitting at road's edge, her back against the stone wall of a merchant's shop. The boy studied her from across the road as they passed her by. She was quite dirty, her clothing in tatters, and despite holding out an empty tin plate to the stream of people passing by, not a single person stopped, nor even met her eyes with theirs.

A few more steps down the road and the boy felt compelled to stop, his eyes fixed on the woman and those ignoring her plight as they passed by her. The Elder stopped beside the boy, and together they continued to watch.

As people would pass the old beggar woman, giving absolutely no notice of her, she would grow angry, which, after a moment, would turn to sadness, and she would wearily lower her tin plate to her lap and put her head down and cry. The boy would see her body shake from the emotion, which was equally ignored by those around her.

But then, she would wipe her face, clear the sadness from her eyes, and lift her plate again to those around her, only to again find no acknowledgement from anyone that passed. This pushed her to anger again, and then sadness, dropping the tin plate to her lap, lowering her head, with new tears upon her face.

A question formulated within the boy at the scene before him: was the old beggar woman angry in her heart, or was she only angry because of people around her ignoring her need for help?

And in watching the plight of the woman, the boy had a profound thought, a thought that for all of the people in the World with needs, there were enough people in the World with help, should they only extend it outward. That, if placed on great scales, the offers of help and kindness and support would outweigh the needs for help and kindness and support. All that was needed was for those with something to offer to add to the scales.

The boy wondered that if this were done, could all of the suffering in the World at the hands of man be eliminated? He believed it could.

The boy removed his pack, opened it, and withdrew the small amount of food that remained within it. With a piece of bread and two small pieces of dried fish in his hand, the boy looked to the Elder with what he wished to do. The Elder smiled, and the boy made his way across the busy road, the Elder beside him, and approached the crying woman quietly.

The boy slowly placed the food onto the dirty plate that lay in the beggar woman's lap, and at this, she raised her eyes to find his.

What the boy saw in her eyes in that instant made clear what drove the anger that he had seen in her actions only moments before.

As the boy began to withdraw his hand slowly, the old beggar woman reached out a dirty hand and took the boy's hand in hers, and she simply held it for a moment. And in looking into the eyes of the old beggar woman, seeing what lay within them, the boy felt that he then saw her with vision of the heart, and not with vision of the eye, and the difference between the two was suddenly very clear to the boy, after which he spoke.

"I know not of what pains you from days prior, nor of what pain may lie in days ahead," said the boy, "but it is my wish that in this moment, on this day, this will help. Your presence here has not gone unnoticed."

The woman smiled, and from that smile, the boy drifted back to his thoughts of the Fabric of People, and how, since all people could be someone to someone, it was not impossible to imagine that she could be a grandmother to him, or a grandmother to someone.

The old woman released his hand, the boy stood, and he and the Elder turned and continued down the road.

And as they walked, the boy felt something else within him.

Memories from the start of the journey returned to him, of the first night with the Elder when the strange, dark traveler visited their camp and the boy shared of his provisions. And how, on the next day, the boy regretted that he had given the dark stranger a share of his limited food, as it would be as the Elder had remarked on it, that the feeding of dark shadows depletes one while it strengthens them.

But although there on the street with the old beggar woman, the boy had again given of his provisions, he now felt very different from when he had given to the dark stranger. His actions with her were not influenced by fear, as they had been with the dark traveler. With the old woman, the boy giving of his provisions came from a different emotion within him, after which the boy actually felt strengthened and sustained. And the wisdom of the Sage returned, that to toil or to give in ways that lifts one is not to toil in vain.

The boy and the Elder continued down the busy road, and it was a few moments later when the boy spoke of the question that had filled his mind when he first saw the anger in the old beggar woman as people passed her by without care.

"Anger is always born of hurt," said the Elder, "and as you have seen, because of this, should always be met as such, with understanding instead of more anger."

The boy thought of times in his own short life when he was greatly angered, and realized that it was as the Elder had said, that the anger in the boy during every one of those moments in his life had in fact come from some form of hurt.

"The remedy for anger is found in the simplest of gestures," said the Elder, "and in helping to heal the hurt in one, you help to heal the anger in one. It is this way in the World as well, for the World is made of people."

"All from a handful of food," said the boy.

"A handful of food to one," replied the Elder, "yet hope to see the light of the next day for another."

And from this, the boy saw the true use and value of things, as he had seen in the journey's events to that point. How the silver figurine of the Colibri bird that he had found on the mountain pass could fetch a coin or two, yet the meaning of it to the grieving boy's Mother in the mountain village was beyond measure. How the key given to them by the grieving Mother was not of gold, yet in freeing the boy Monk from his cage, had value that could not be matched. And how the simple boat of the dying Father on the far side of the Sea would fulfill the wish for both he and his son across the waters, and would finally close the distance between them after so many lost seasons.

And although the boy no longer possessed any of the items at that moment, they had nonetheless enriched him for having passed them along and realized their true value.

It was to the boy that the true value of things was in what they could do to help the Fabric of People become the Tapestry of Spirit.

It was then that the boy's thoughts returned to what the Sage had said about all things being spun from a single strand, and he wondered if the single strand was at the heart of transforming the Fabric of People to the Tapestry of Spirit.

❧ 19 ❧

In was late afternoon when the boy and the Elder followed a turn in the crowded road, continued for a short distance, turned back and joined an even larger road, and finally glimpsed the great stone amphitheatre ahead of them.

Even in the distance, at the end of the road they traveled, the amphitheatre towered high above the surrounding rooftops, and the boy was in amazement at how massive it must be, if from even this distance, it dwarfed all around it. His mind drifted back to the enormity of the sprawling, curved tree that the Sage lived beneath, and the boy wondered what wisdom might exist within the amphitheatre, as had existed within the tree.

A short while later, they reached the enormous stone structure. Its towering, circular walls rose high into the sky, ornate with countless carved figures of men and animals, and rows of written characters and symbols, most of which the boy had never seen.

As people crowded about the structure, the boy wandered its vast perimeter, amazed at the stories that were told and the wisdom that was shared in its carvings and characters, all inscribed on its surface in great, wide, curved stone panels.

And in the variety of writings and images inscribed in the stone, the boy felt as if they represented the variety of people and beliefs, from various lands both near and far, that had come to this place, and still did, judging by the diversity of the people streaming through its great, stone entryways.

As the boy and the Elder stepped through one of the many long, crowded, entryways that led into the great amphitheatre, the boy was again astonished at what he saw once inside.

At the center of the enormous amphitheatre was a vast, circular floor, made of large, square slabs of stone butted end-to-end across its entirety. From the center of the stone floor and radiating outward, there were rows and rows of ornate, curved stone benches, forming concentric circles that repeated from the center of the floor to its edges. The radiating circles of seating were divided by four walkways that ran from the edge of the amphitheatre floor to its center, effectively quartering the entire floor and its stone benches, with each section being aligned to each of the four cardinal directions.

Along the entirety of the outer edge of the circular floor began rows and rows of simpler stone benches, continuing to circle the stone floor as they rose up in concentric circles to the very tops of the walls of the massive amphitheatre. While the stone benches on the floor of the mighty structure were empty, the countless rows of benches for the spectators that rose up around them were not, with hardly an area of the amphitheatre where open benches could be seen.

The boy simply stood, surveying the crowded amphitheatre, having never seen such diversity displayed before him. There were skin colors and facial features of every type, clothing styles and fabrics from tribes and clans across the World, and languages in the air of all variety, the entire collection of which filled the amphitheatre, from the floor at its center to the top of its massive outer walls.

And in looking across the vast collection of diverse humanity that seemed to gently sway and undulate before him by its activity, it appeared to the boy as if the entire amphitheatre, the Circle of Beliefs, was itself alive.

The Elder led the boy up several rows to one of the few benches with seating available, and once seated, the boy could clearly see the entirety of the vast, circular floor below them.

In a moment, there began the streaming of four groups of people down the four walkways on the amphitheatre floor, distinctive from each other by their clothing and its color, and the types of people that seemed to move together toward each of the four quarters of bench areas.

Soon, they were all seated as groups in each of the quarters except for four individuals, each standing innermost toward the center of the great circle and at the front of the groups that they had entered with. These were the representatives of each of the four groups.

At the front of each of the large groups to the North, West, and South stood elderly men, Holy Men, with ornately trimmed robes of different colors than the other groups to distinguish them apart. All of their followers seated behind them on the amphitheatre floor, from the center to its edge, wore clothing of similar color and decoration.

But the group from the East was noticeably different, only half in number as the other groups, and dressed in simple and varied, yet colorful clothing. And at the innermost part of the smaller group stood an elderly woman, dressed in a simple, drab robe, a long braid of silver hair hanging down behind her.

The boy and the Elder had found the Wholy Woman.

With the Sun low in the sky to the West, its light crossed over the Western wall of the amphitheatre and illuminated only the Wholy Woman and those assembled behind her from the East. The other three groups on the amphitheatre floor were in shadow, and despite the grand clothing worn by the groups from the North, South, and West, the simple, illuminated appearance of the small group from the East made them appear much more alive and remarkable in the light of the setting Sun.

Then the gathering commenced.

First, the elderly Holy Man from the North spoke of the virtues and certainties of his group's beliefs, and his followers behind him cheered when he pointed out the deficiencies or incorrectness of the other surrounding beliefs, which incited the followers in the other groups to shout back in anger.

Only the Wholy Woman from the East and those assembled behind her sat in silence.

At the end of the Northern leader's proclamations, he asked those in the other groups seated on the floor, as well as those seated around the amphitheatre, to join them and follow them back to the North.

When he had finished speaking, the elderly Holy Man from the West then spoke of the virtues and certainties of his group's beliefs, eliciting cheers from his followers as he condemned the other groups for their beliefs and falsehoods, which incited the followers in the other groups to retort back in anger.

Again, only the Wholy Woman from the East and those assembled behind her sat in silence.

At the end of the Western leader's proclamations, he asked those in the other groups seated on the floor, as well as those seated around the amphitheatre, to join them and follow them back to the West.

When he had finished speaking, the elderly Holy Man from the South then spoke of the greatness and correctness of his group's beliefs, drawing cheers from his followers as he mocked the falseness of the other groups and their beliefs, which incited the followers in the other groups to rise and respond in anger.

And again, only the Wholy Woman from the East and those assembled behind her sat in silence.

At the end of the Southern leader's proclamations, he too asked those from the other groups seated on the floor, as well as those seated in the amphitheatre, to join them and follow them back to the South.

Eventually, he too stopped speaking, and there was a long silence while the three groups that had already spoken waited for the Wholy Woman from the East to speak, which she did.

"It is my wish that instead of pulling away from each other in this great amphitheater, that we may join together in its center," she said. "I will not speak against you, for to do so would be to speak against myself. Where you only see differences, I only see things shared."

The three Holy Men and their followers were confused at the statements, and soon their rumbling became angry shouts and demands for explanations for the beliefs of the woman from the East.

The Wholy Woman raised her arms and the amphitheater eventually fell quiet for her to continue.

"Over the generations, God has sent several of his most special messengers to us. Because they were sent to different regions and in different generations, they spoke in different ways, but all were of the same, and sent to teach us."

"You do not read your own texts correctly, nor ours!" came angry replies.

"I have read all texts, and in them, I see only the same message told in different ways. But beyond whatever texts are written, the essence of Spirit exits within all of us. It transcends the written or spoken word," said the woman.

The crowds became agitated again, but settled as the Wholy Woman again raised her arms and resumed speaking.

"Just as the outside walls of this amphitheatre bear the languages and likenesses of many, many peoples, they are all still inscribed on a single structure," she began. "While each of you has chosen to follow a different messenger from God, they each were sent from the one God. Each of God's messengers is a Thread of Destiny from the Tapestry of Spirit," she said, "with their messages meant to bind us together, not unravel us."

In the boy's ears, the words spoken by the Wholy Woman were as those spoken by the Elder days earlier when they first began the crossing of the Sea, and it was indeed as she said, that the messages that the boy and the Elder then carried would connect them to strangers across the waters, making them strangers no more.

At the words from the Wholy Woman, the groups and their Holy Men leaders again unleashed their anger and denial at such statements and beliefs, shouting and proclaiming their set of beliefs as the lone truthful one, and mocking the foreign things that the Wholy Woman spoke of.

She raised her arms to the air and the groups eventually fell quiet enough again for her to make a final statement.

"The division of the people of the World under separate banners of belief is man's doing, not God's."

This further incensed the Holy Men and their followers, and their collective rage was then in the open air, effectively ending the gathering. Each of them and their groups stormed from the great floor and toward the hallways that led to the outside of the amphitheatre, and once outside, led their followers back to the North, West, and South, from whence they had come.

The rows of spectators then began to disperse and leave the amphitheatre as well. Only the Wholy Woman and the small group behind her remained seated, and calm.

And as the Elder and the boy sat as the people around them began to leave, the boy saw the similarity between what the Wholy Woman had said and the words spoken by the Sage. That, as it appeared to the boy, it was the World of men that seemed to demand a complex answer of intellect to a question of something so pure and simple as the Spirit of the World. And that the World of men so often prosecuted the search for Spirit with such blind vigor, that they neglected to see its very presence before them in each rising of the Sun.

As the amphitheatre cleared, the Wholy Woman led her small, quiet, and orderly group back toward the hallways that would lead to the outside of the amphitheatre and to the East.

The Elder and the boy began their way down through the clearing rows of stone benches, finally able to approach the Wholy Woman just as she and her group were outside of the amphitheatre and in a busy road.

"Greetings," said the boy, to which she smiled, stopped to face he and the Elder, and gestured in return. And from the simple sincerity in the Wholy Woman's greeting, the boy felt truly acknowledged.

"We carry word of someone who, long ago, was taken from you," began the boy.

The Wholy Woman tilted her head in interest. "Yes?" she asked.

"Javell sends word that he is well and is sharing the wisdom of the Tapestry of Spirit," said the boy.

At this, the Wholy Woman smiled broadly, one of relief and then joy.

"It has been many seasons since his disappearance," she said, "and I am grateful to hear of his well-being."

And in that moment, the boy felt as if he were a strand that connected Javell and the Wholy Woman, despite the distance between them. And in thinking of it further, the boy realized that it had been so throughout his entire journey, that he had been a strand between the grieving Mother, the boy Monk freed by her key, the dying Father, and his lost Son across the Sea. The messages that the boy had carried between them, had in fact served to connect them.

"It would please me greatly to know more of Javell," said the Wholy Woman to the boy and the Elder. "Please, accompany me to our village for a meal this evening and a place for the night. It is just outside of the city to the East."

And with that, the boy and the Elder resumed walking with the Wholy Woman and her group, out of the city and toward the East. As they walked, the boy and the Elder shared with her their encounter with Javell and his captor. They shared of his freedom from the cage by the key that they were given by the grieving Mother in the mountains to the West.

"Destiny Threads crossing to reveal the Tapestry of Spirit," said the Wholy Woman with a contented smile.

And as they walked together, and as the Sun neared the horizon to the West, the boy also told of his own journey East with the Elder.

"And you are to meet the Mage," said the Wholy Woman, surprising the boy at her knowledge of something he had not mentioned.

She simply smiled and said, "Those that journey East, in following their Destiny Thread to a meeting with the Mage, are very clear to my eyes, for it is these people, and those who have already met the Mage and returned to the Tapestry of Spirit, that form the village that we now travel to."

And it was then that the boy realized that it was she that the Sage had said would show the boy the way of the many, and the boy then found himself in great curiosity about the village that they would soon reach.

❧ 20 ❧

The Sun had just set when they reached the communal village of the Wholy Woman. It was a small, simple village of simple cottages, with small, hanging lanterns throughout that were just being lit as the sky turned to darkness.

As the group led by the Wholy Woman returned to the village, people appeared, approached and greeted them back, and were especially friendly to the boy and the Elder. And with this welcome as they entered the village, the boy felt a great calm being gently pulled over him, as if a warm blanket on a cold night. It was similar to the feeling that he had had on the Sea the morning following the storm, when the oars returned to them.

And it then occurred to the boy that being among all of the people of the village, people that, as the Wholy Woman had said, were of the Tapestry of Spirit, was what gave him this feeling. It was as the Elder had said about being with the Sage, that being around those that had returned to the Tapestry of Spirit were the better for it.

The Wholy Woman led the boy and the Elder into the center of the modest village, to a small gathering area where an evening meal was being prepared at a large, central fire pit, around which gathered a diverse group of people, even more so than what the boy had seen in the Circle of Beliefs.

They were of different colors, different ages, different languages being shared, but all somehow connected. The crowds of the large port city were the same in their appearance, but different in that they seemed all alone, not connected. But here, in the communal village, the feeling was very different to the boy. There seemed to exist great respect and care for each other as they interacted.

The Wholy Woman could see the effect that the village was having on the boy, and she spoke.

"They see the Spirit within each other and themselves, in all things. When they look upon another, they see not another, but themselves, as if a reflection in a mirror." And the boy's thoughts drifted to his dream of the girl in the frame.

The boy and the Elder were served a delicious meal of herbs and roots, after which the Wholy Woman explained more of their beliefs.

"We live by a simple trine of principles," she said.

The boy listened attentively for what was at the heart of the way of the many, and the Wholy Woman continued.

"The first is to ensure that we are in constant recognition of the single strand from which every Destiny Thread is spun, and because of that, is shared by all," she said and smiled, taking note of the boy's overt curiosity, as it was the same thing that the Sage had explained to him many evenings prior, only to leave him without an answer as to what the single strand was.

"The single strand, from which all is spun, enables all things in the World, and with this uppermost in our hearts, we are true to ourselves and to each other," added the Wholy Woman.

The boy was anxious for her to identify what it was, which she realized, and then smiled.

"The meeting of the Mage will make this clear to you," she said, to the boy's chagrin.

"The second principle is that each of us are healers," continued the Wholy Woman. "For within each of us exists the ability to ease the suffering of another, and in easing the suffering of another, we can help in their healing, and in healing the one, we can heal the World.

The Wholy Woman smiled at the attentiveness of the boy before she continued.

"And the third of our principles is quite simple," she said. "With the first and second utmost in our minds, we simply are. And in doing so, we live within the Tapestry of Spirit."

The third principle resonated within the boy, as it was the simplicity that the Sage spoke of.

"This village is the Tapestry of Spirit lived," added the Wholy Woman.

And this too surfaced memories in the boy of what the Sage had said about the mighty, curved tree that he lived beneath, that it also was the Tapestry of Spirit lived.

The boy reflected on the trine of principles that were just explained to him.

"Is that why you go to the Circle of Beliefs?" asked the boy, "To share of this trine?"

"Yes, to share of our beliefs, beliefs that those around us are brothers and sisters, regardless of what clan or tribe or region of the World that they may come from."

The boy thought of how the Wholy Woman's view was that of the World, and not just a part of it.

"It is a major difference between us and others," said the Wholy Woman, "for the way of the Tapestry of Spirit is to be drawn to realize it through unity, not pushed toward, or from it, because of division. But, things require time. A seed planted at dusk not does not yield a tree by dawn."

Her words were again as the Sage and the boy Monk had said, and it again amazed the boy at how prevalent this wisdom seemed to be now that he sought it.

"There are those that believe that life is a thread of misery, with only a few moments of joy during its length. Others believe that life is a thread of joy with only a few moments of misery during its length," said the Wholy Woman. "The people here believe that every moment is of value and necessary, and is enjoyed as such, regardless of how it may be defined."

Just then, a small, smiling child, a dark-skinned girl who had been watching the boy all evening, shyly approached and said unfamiliar words to the boy. He turned to the Wholy Woman.

"It is a greeting in her native language," said the Wholy Woman. "To repeat it back to her is customary."

So the boy tried to repeat what he had heard, to which the girl smiled and happily returned back across the central area to her waiting Mother who smiled at the boy. The boy smiled back, and a moment later, looked up to the night sky, to the new moon, and felt himself new again among the people of the village.

And from the night sky, the boy's gaze dropped to the fire before him, and while looking into the fire, a glint from beyond it caught the boy's eye, and he looked up to see a woman sitting alone on the other side of the fire. For all the conversation going on around her, she was the only one that sat alone and in silence. She was twice the boy's age, and was simply smiling at him, a pleasant, comforting smile, and the boy's impression of her in that instant was that she was at peace.

The boy smiled back, and then returned his gaze to the fire. After a moment, his thoughts returned to the glint that had caught his eye, but as he looked up again and across the fire, the woman was gone.

The rest of the evening was spent with the Wholy Woman and the rest of those that lived there, and the boy freely conversed with all of them. He felt very at ease with them, and felt as if he were a part of the group, that he did not feel like an outsider.

And it was the group that surrounded him that felt both like a Fabric of People and a Tapestry of Spirit.

Later in the evening, when the sharing around the fire was over, the Wholy Woman took the boy and the Elder to a small, empty cottage where they would sleep for the night. It was not long before the boy had fallen to sleep.

Sometime during the night, the boy stirred, not knowing why. Looking over, he noticed the Elder was gone, with the door to the small cottage open just a crack. The boy rose, stepped to the door, and opened it slowly.

There, a few steps in front of the cottage and with his back to the door, the Elder stood motionless, facing East, his head tilted upward toward the new moon in the dark sky overhead. The boy remained quiet in the doorway of the cottage, choosing not to interrupt the Elder, for while he did not know of what he did, it seemed to him as if the Elder had great purpose in standing there under the night sky.

The boy quietly closed the cottage door, returned to his bed of straw, and went back to sleep.

When the boy awoke early the next morning, he was again alone in the cottage. He rose, stepped to the door that was still just slightly ajar, and opened it, again finding the Elder standing where he had during the night when the boy stirred. Only now, with the moon gone from view in the dawn sky, the Elder stood facing the glow of the rising Sun to the East.

The boy's curiosity had the better of him, and as he quietly approached the Elder from the side, he noticed that the Elder's eyes were closed, and after a moment of the boy remaining still and quiet beside him, the Elder opened his eyes and turned to the boy.

"We are nearing the conclusion of your journey," said the Elder, which caught the boy by surprise and he smiled broadly, excitement filling his heart.

But in that moment, another emotion came to him. While the excitement of meeting the Mage and realizing his return to the Tapestry of Spirit was to provide answers to the unspoken questions that had grown within the boy for the past several seasons, it was tempered by a sadness over the journey itself coming to an end.

Yet it was the sadness that the boy was somehow able to see as a good thing, as it meant that he had come to enjoy the journey as much as the promise of its destination. Such was the wisdom from the stepping stones across the river earlier in the journey.

Then the words of the Sage returned to him, those of one's Destiny Thread being lived, not reached, and with that, the boy realized that while the journey to meet the Mage may conclude, the journey of living his Destiny Thread was only beginning.

The Wholy Woman appeared, greeted the boy and the Elder, and led them back to the center of the village where people were gathered as the sky lightened, and they all shared a morning meal. And the interaction with the villagers during the meal was just as fulfilling as it had been the night before, the boy again feeling at ease in their presence and a part of something bigger.

Afterwards, the small girl who had greeted the boy in her native tongue the night prior appeared, the boy's full pack upon her back and dwarfing her, it having been filled with provisions by the villagers. Being a small child, it was all she could do to walk the filled pack over to the boy without falling, yet she smiled all along the way. The villagers thoroughly enjoyed her commitment to the task, and upon reaching the boy, he helped remove the load she carried, and she gave him a gentle kiss upon the cheek and then scurried off.

The Wholy Woman appeared next to the boy, holding something small in the fingers of one hand.

"For you," she said, extending her arm, to which the boy extended an open hand, into which the Wholy Woman placed a small, heart-shaped, crimson stone.

"It is a Heart Stone," she said, "and it will keep your course true beyond this journey."

The boy took the item from her hand and studied it, noting how smooth and worn it was, as the Wholy Woman continued.

"As with all Heart Stones, this one has been used by generations of those following their Destiny Threads and living within the Tapestry of Spirit, and as such, it carries with it the journeys and wisdom of many, many others."

The boy was confused, as he had the Elder as a guide to meet the Mage and return to the Tapestry of Spirit.

"The journey you are on is to meet the Mage," explained the Wholy Woman. "But beyond this meeting, the Heart Stone will help you to continue to follow your Destiny Thread and to remain living within the Tapestry of Spirit."

For the first time since his journey with the Elder began, the boy considered the probability that after reaching the Mage, the Elder may not remain in his life. It was a sad realization for the boy, but given the Elder's purpose in his life, it seemed likely that it was to be so. He looked to the Elder and managed a hollow smile, which the Elder returned sympathetically, confirming to the boy that what he had just realized was the truth about their remaining time together.

The boy's attention returned to the Heart Stone in his hand, and the Wholy Woman.

"How is the wisdom of the stone summoned?" asked the boy.

"With closed eyes and a quiet mind, hold it closely to your heart as you ask for guidance about your course in following your Destiny Thread. When you have prepared yourself for an answer, drop the stone before you," she explained. "When you open your eyes, you will see the course."

"And how will I know when to use it?" asked the boy.

"There may, at times, be great influences upon you to stray from your Destiny Thread. You will know this when your vision of the eye does not align to your vision of the heart," the Wholy Woman said. "In those times, look to the Heart Stone to keep your course true. But remember this," she added, "it merely tells you what you already know, what you have always known, and because of that, you will one day no longer need its guidance, as by then you will know how to follow your own heart without fail."

"And when that day comes?" asked the boy.

"You must pass the Heart Stone on to another who is in search of their own Destiny Thread, and instruct them as I instruct you now," replied the Wholy Woman. "It is the way it has been done for generations."

The boy again studied the smooth stone in his hand, and imagined how many hands had held it before him, and how many it had helped. And with that thought, the boy felt that there in his hand, he held many Destiny Threads all at once.

"Then I will honor it as such," said the boy, and placed the stone in his pack.

And with that, the Wholy Woman smiled, stepped forward and embraced the boy, and as she held him, it was to the boy as if he were held snugly in a warm blanket, one from which he did not want to part.

She then stepped to the Elder and they embraced, and as they embraced, there were soft words spoken between them, words so soft that the boy could not hear or understand, yet he could tell that there was much feeling in them.

And as their embrace continued, the boy looked at the villagers gathered around them, and at the edge, saw the smiling woman that he had noticed the night prior, and again, he found her to be simply looking at him and smiling as she had before.

But it was in the morning light that the boy saw something that he did not see clearly the night prior. For around her neck hung a silver figurine of a Colibri on a leather string, and the boy wondered if it was she who had stayed with the grieving Mother and her lost son many, many seasons ago.

The Elder and the Wholy Woman stepped apart, and the Elder picked up the full pack from the ground and handed it to the boy.

"The pack is now yours to carry," said the Elder, and the boy slung the pack over his shoulders and the two of them left the village and continued toward the East.

As they walked that morning, the Elder spoke to the boy on a subject that he had not spoken on before.

"Your Mother takes pride in you, and in your journey," he said.

The statement surprised the boy, as he had never spoken of her to the Elder, yet there was comfort for the boy in what the Elder said, for he spoke in the present tense.

"Three evenings from tonight, you will reach the conclusion of this journey," said the Elder. "But before that, she will once again be in your presence."

The boy stopped, the Elder a step later. So moved was the boy that he took pause, but instead of immediately seeking to know more of exactly where and when it would be, another feeling made itself known within him. It was a feeling of simple belief that it was to be so, just as had been everything else that the Elder had told him of along their journey. The demonstration of Spirit need not be pursued relentlessly, the boy thought. All that was needed was to look with open eyes, and to have belief.

By late morning, the boy found himself again thinking of what he believed to be little remaining time with the Elder, which saddened him, prompting him to speak.

"Will our Destiny Threads remain together after I meet the Mage?" asked the boy tentatively, wanting the truth yet also fearing it.

The Elder knew what answer the boy's heart was hoping for, and so, after a thoughtful pause, the Elder replied simply, "I will always journey with you, in one way or another."

☙ 21 ❧

Just before mid-day, as they traversed open terrain through sparse patches of knee-high grasses, they were surprised to come upon a deer. It lay perfectly still in the middle of a small patch of grass, its head only partly raised, an effort of concealment failed.

Upon seeing the animal in the grass, and it seeing them, the Elder and the boy froze, and the animal made no attempt to rise and flee. This puzzled the boy, for the animal could easily outrun them.

The Elder, the boy, and the deer all remained motionless, simply eyeing each other for a moment, before the deer slowly lowered its head to its front legs, its eyes remaining on the boy and the Elder as it did so.

At this, the Elder took a slow step toward it, then another, with the boy doing the same, while the animal remained where it was watching their approach.

Upon nearing the deer, the boy saw the reason for its behavior: an unsettling, bloody gash along its abdomen that had exposed the insides of the animal and pooled bright red blood onto the grass beneath it. Behind the wounded animal and from the East, a meandering trail of blood marred the otherwise pristine scenery.

As the boy and the Elder knelt beside the animal, it began to tremble in fear, yet remained on the ground, making no attempt to move. The Elder took the boy's hand and slowly placed it on the side of the deer, near the base of its neck, to which the boy immediately felt the trembling of the animal cease.

The words that the Elder would speak next were so soft as to almost be imperceptible.

"The Spirit of all animals and all people can depart in peace if helped by another, and it is touch that enables this to happen."

It was clear to the boy that he was to remain in contact with the deer until its passing, which, from its wounds, seemed imminent.

As the boy remained by the side of the animal with his hand upon it, he became more aware of the deer, as if becoming a part of it. He could feel her breathing, her warmth, her pain and fear, and in a sense, the comfort to her that his touch provided.

"To ease the passing of another is to experience the Tapestry of Spirit," said the Elder softly, and with that, the deer passed. And when it passed, the boy felt something pass through him, an essence aloft, and having had the feeling pass through him, the boy was profoundly moved.

It occurred to the boy in that moment that while death was a certainty, life was not, and memories returned to him, with wishes that he somehow could have been with his Mother, to provide peace and comfort in her final moments, as he had the deer.

The boy kept his hand on the animal for a moment longer, lost in what he had just been a part of, as well as the memories from the past, only withdrawing when the warmth of the deer receded beneath his touch.

"The passage of time in the World cannot be controlled," said the Elder softly, as if directly addressing the regret from the past that had been stirred within the boy. "Just as the timing of some events cannot."

And the Elder's words regarding the event from the boy's past were the first of their kind to provide the boy with any sense of real comfort.

❧ 22 ❧

By early afternoon, the course East had led the boy and the Elder toward a dense forest. As they approached, a large, black, tusked boar suddenly appeared at its edge, to which the Elder immediately shuffled the boy behind him. The boar charged out toward them, stopping abruptly some ten paces from where the Elder and the boy stood, stomping and snorting and studying them with black, insidious eyes, its short tail flipping about angrily. Then, as quickly as it had appeared, it turned and stormed back into the dense forest and was out of sight.

Even though the boy felt fear at the appearance of the animal, he held conviction of his course. Back on the snowy mountain pass, with the darkened passageway before him, the boy sought a change to his course to prevent confronting it, but this time, the boy sought no such alternate course. While earlier in the journey he had questioned the course when danger and challenges arose, this time his mind remained silent, steadfast, and to the East. The boy simply turned to the Elder, who turned to look at him, and it was clear to the Elder that the boy was ready to enter the forest.

As the Elder led the boy into the forest, they entered a lush, canopied landscape, and before long, they were deep into a dense mix of trees, ground cover, large rocks, and vines crawling all about, with only scant shards of light from the Sun finding their way through the thick foliage above and to the forest floor at their feet. And as they progressed into the forest, the sounds of the life within it became clear.

For what seemed an immeasurably long duration, they cautiously worked their way through the forest, with the Elder pausing regularly to listen to the sounds of the forest: birds in song, animals foraging, even the insects tilling the soil, it seemed, could be heard. Then, the Elder and the boy would continue on, only to pause again a short while later to listen again.

Not a word was said between them during their journey through the forest, as the boy sensed the heightened awareness of the Elder and knew by his behavior that this was a treacherous place.

As the rest of the day passed, and with the thick canopy of foliage continually above them, the boy lost all sense of the position of the Sun in the sky, but surmised that the Sun must by then surely be on its path toward the horizon in the West.

Suddenly, the Elder paused, and quickly crouched to the ground. The boy did the same, crouching closely behind the Elder. The Elder remained motionless for a moment, then a moment longer, scanning the forest around them.

And as they crouched together in silence there on the forest floor, the sounds of the forest oddly began to fade. The sounds of the birds, animals, and insects slowly began to retreat from around them, finally to be absent altogether, leaving only the faintest sound of running water somewhere in the distance ahead of them to the East.

The Elder turned his head to face the direction from which they had come, and suddenly, the Elder rose, grasping the boy by the arm and jerking him to his feet, both of them ending up in a stumbling sprint to the East.

"Into the trees!" shouted the Elder, and he flung the boy ahead of him toward a nearby tree.

As the frightened boy reached the base of the tree, he heard from behind them the approaching thunder of hooves on the forest floor, and he could almost feel the earth beneath him trembling.

The boy desperately grasped and clawed at the slippery vines and trunk of the tree, making his way upward as the thunder of the hooves continued their approach.

"Up! Up!" shouted the Elder from below him, as the panicked boy climbed his way toward the lower of two large branches that forked from opposite sides of the trunk of the tree, some distance from the forest floor below.

As the boy reached the lowest stout branch, he managed to work one leg over and beyond it, reaching his arms around the wide trunk of the tree as he did so, with he and the pack upon his back being wedged into the safety of a natural saddle that the branch forking from the tree had created.

The boy then turned to look for the Elder, expecting to find him close behind, scurrying up the trunk of the tree to the safety of the second branch. But to the boy's shock, the Elder was not on the tree, and was making no attempt to climb it. He simply stood on the ground at the base of the tree, looking up at the boy.

From the direction they had run from, the boy found what they had so desperately fled, and what he saw truly terrified him.

An enormous boar, dwarfing the one they had encountered at the edge of the forest earlier in the day, raced toward the Elder standing alone at the base of the tree. The animal was massive, its shoulders as high as a man, with a huge, ugly head hideously adorned with enormous tusks that curled up and around in a most menacing manner.

The boy was without words, and looked down desperately to the Elder who remained standing at the base of the tree below him. The eyes of the boy met the eyes of the Elder, but the Elder simply showed a calm, contented smile, as if nothing else existed in the World but the boy, and he remained motionless at the base of the tree.

And as the charging boar approached the base of the tree, its fury focused solely on the Elder standing motionless before it, the boy screamed.

"Nooo!"

The word was still in the air, with the boy's eyes locked onto those of the calm Elder, as the boar reached him. With a powerful thrash of its enormous head, the curved tusks tore into the Elder from the side, crushing and bending his left upper arm in a most hideous fashion, the force of which drove the Elder's own head down and into violent contact with the skull of the boar. The Elder's body was launched into the air and toward two large slabs of rock nearby, his limp body falling between them and into a natural crevice created by their proximity to each other.

"Nooo!" screamed the boy again in horror as the boar immediately charged to where the Elder was thrown, and upon reaching the rock crevice, the boar began to viciously batter away at it with its massive, vile head.

At this, the boy again screamed, over and over, in a desperate but unrealistic hope that it would stop the brutality before him. But his screams went unheard over the din of the enormous tusks scraping and slashing at the rocks, and the skull smashing against the crevice where the still motionless Elder lay crumpled, protected.

The boy continued screaming, and finally, with a snort, the panting beast raised its head and stepped backward away from the rock crevice, having made no progress at inflicting further injury to the Elder, and turned toward the boy in the tree, giving him full view to the result of its violence.

Its head had been torn and bloodied by its blind fury, and blood now ran so freely down the front of its skull as if to appear a solid stream. A grotesque froth, spattered with crimson, bubbled from its mouth and nose with every enraged pant, and its tusks were chipped and scuffed, one now missing a tip entirely, from its violent assault on the unyielding rocks.

It stood, in all of its ugliness, glaring at the boy high in the tree who had now stopped yelling. The beast turned and looked to where the motionless body of the Elder remained wedged between the two slabs of rock. It then looked back to the boy in the tree and began to trot toward him, causing the boy to tighten his grip around the trunk.

The bloodied beast reached the base of the tree and stood, glaring up at the boy with its black eyes, the odor of its blood now filling the boy's nose as he looked down upon it from the safety of the tree. The panting beast stood for a moment, its violent intentions toward the boy clear within its eyes, then, with an emphatic snort, blew blood and froth up onto the tree and the boy, and it turned and trotted off into the forest to the West from where it had come, leaving a trail of blood behind it on the green forest floor.

The boy remained in the safety of the tree, and from his vantage point, he saw the boar move up and over a rise in the forest floor, and then was gone.

As the sounds of the forest began to slowly return, the boy's attention was back to the Elder, whose body remained motionless between the bloodied rocks in the distance. The boy's eyes were fixed on the Elder, hoping for some kind of movement, but there was none.

The boy cautiously began to make his way down the trunk of the tree, intently listening and turning his head frequently to scan for signs of the beast's return.

Once on the ground, the boy quickly and quietly made his way toward the Elder, feeling nausea within him as he approached the violent scene: the deep hoof gouges in the soil surrounding the rocks, the blood and froth everywhere, the scrapes around the bloodied crevice, and finally, the crumpled, bloodied figure of the Elder, his body contorted and twisted within the crevice.

The boy began to cry silently as he crouched down close to the crevice and peered in at the condition of the Elder. His face was turned inward, away from the boy, and his upper left arm was badly gashed and exposed, the two ends of the snapped bone jutting outward toward the boy. His entire left side was bloody from horrific gashes across his ribs, the flesh laid open to reveal pieces of broken bones within.

The panicked boy continued to cry silently, frantic but not knowing what to do next.

Then, to his surprise, came the faintest groan from the crevice, and the boy knew what difficult thing needed to be done.

With the gentlest touch that he could summon, the boy began to pull the broken body from the crevice, his hands quickly becoming wet with the warm blood of the Elder. As the boy freed the semi-conscious Elder, his head swung around toward the boy to reveal a horribly bloodied face from a great gash on the left side of the Elder's head, a match to the rest of the hideous wounds that turned the boy's stomach as he pulled the Elder from the rocks.

With the Elder freed, the boy strained and then lifted the mangled body of the Elder up into his arms and proceeded to carry him forward and East, toward the sound of the running water that they had heard just ahead of them when the forest had been silent.

The forest began to thin, the canopy above became less dense, and soon thereafter, the boy had crossed over the forest's edge, just beyond which flowed a river.

His strength sapped, the breathless, panicked boy lowered the Elder to the ground and then collapsed beside him.

Now, with the Elder laid out on the ground beside him, the boy had full view to all of the violent deformities of the Elder's mangled body, and the boy was horrified all over again.

Just then, the Elder's eyes began to flutter and he managed a pained, muffled cough, his breathing labored through a nose and mouth that both bled. The Elder's eyes slowly opened just enough for him to see, and the boy noticed that his entire left eye had filled with blood, leaving no white visible. The Elder became vaguely aware of the boy's presence and looked slowly to him.

The boy's mind was a blur of horror, sadness and despair.

The Elder's gaze, a calm, quiet gaze even then, remained on the boy for a moment, and the Elder slowly raised his trembling, bloodied right hand for the boy to take, which he did gently.

They simply held hands for a moment, their eyes in each others, the boy feeling of the Elder, and with a final, labored breath, the life left the Elder's eyes.

And in that final instant with the Elder's hand in his, the boy had done for the Elder what he had done for the deer earlier in the day, and as the life left the Elder's body, the boy felt the essence of the Elder pass through him.

The boy leaned over, gently embraced the lifeless body of the Elder, and wept, for the boy knew why it was that the Elder did nothing to flee from the beast. That his sacrifice would be what would save the boy, and that his words of the boy's journey would indeed be true, that the boy would be the only one that could complete his journey.

After a few moments, the boy pulled back from the Elder, now the both of them an awful, bloody mess, the boy with much of the Elder's blood on his hands, arms, face and clothing. And as the boy looked at the Elder's condition, he thought that it was not as he should look, as odd as the thought was to have at that moment. So, the softly weeping boy rose and then lifted the Elder's body up into his arms and carried him toward the river.

Stepping into the warm, gently flowing water, with his fear of crossing water no longer within him, the boy carried the Elder to the center of the river. With the water at the boy's waist, he paused, and with great gentleness he slowly lowered the body of the Elder into the water, allowing it to wash the signs of violence from him, cleansing him. And as the boy submerged the Elder's body, the flow of the water gently closed the Elder's lifeless eyes and washed the blood from his face.

The boy then crossed the remainder of the river, and once he had emerged on the other side, he gently laid the Elder on the ground. The boy took off his pack and dropped it to the ground, then knelt beside the Elder and simply remained there by his side, crying quietly, his weary and frightened mind filled with despair and sadness.

As the light of the Sun began to leave the sky, the exhausted boy's mind became numb and indifferent to all around him. There was no journey, no tomorrow, and no seasons ahead of him. There was no light upon what any of that might hold, for all of the boy's thoughts were ruled by the sadness that now fully consumed him.

For while the Elder had taught him much during their journey together, the boy was still a boy that had been forced into the World of men, and because of that, he still had need for comfort as a boy would in such a time.

He lay down next to the Elder, placed his hand over his, and quietly wept. And soon, without intending to, he drifted into sleep.

❧ 23 ❧

Sunlight woke the boy the following morning, his waking thoughts still of the tragedy of the prior day. But as the boy cleared his eyes, the Elder was gone. There was no sign of him at all, nor where he had been on the ground near the boy. The boy stood and looked about, but there was no trace of the Elder anywhere, or any sign that he had ever been. The boy found his own footprints as they emerged from the river and muddied the soil the day before, but there was nothing aside from that.

The boy sat down on the ground where he had slept and sat for a long, long while, his mind consumed with a jumble of thoughts and feelings. He was perplexed at the disappearance of the Elder, still horrified at the gruesomeness of his death, and uncertain as to what would become of his journey.

As the Sun continued its slow journey across the morning sky, the boy continued to sit, and it was only when the Sun had reached a position directly overhead and cast no shadows that words came to the boy's thoughts. They were words that spoke of Nature and the balance of things, and how it is the way of Nature to find balance. That all things are born of Nature, and that all things eventually return to Nature. And to the boy, the question of where the Elder had gone was answered: he had simply somehow returned to Nature.

And with that simple, unexpected conclusion, the boy was suddenly and oddly at ease, and thoughts of his journey began to return to him, for he realized that he must continue and finish the journey alone, as the Elder had said he would.

The boy stood and looked East, but in doing so, felt doubt rise up within him, for while East had always been the course up to then, the boy thought, how would he know if it were to remain so? Or was the Elder to guide them in a different direction in the coming days, had he still been with him? How would the boy know how to continue on to the meeting of the Mage? The Elder had said that it would be several more days before he reached the conclusion of the journey, and the boy feared that over that amount of distance, he could become very lost if his course were not true.

But as the fears to his course filled him, the boy suddenly and simply decided not to heed them, replacing them instead with a different feeling that had served the boy well along his journey: belief. For with belief, the boy felt that he had all that was needed, and that the course would make itself known to him.

And with this belief, he was suddenly reminded of what the Wholy Woman had given him, something that could help to point his course along his Destiny Thread in times of uncertainty.

He opened his pack and removed the Heart Stone, the words of the Wholy Woman sounding within him as to how to call upon its wisdom and guidance.

The boy clutched the stone in his hand, held it close to his heart, and with closed eyes and the quietest mind that he could summon, thought about what it was that he wished above all else. He thought about all that he had seen and been a part of on his journey. He thought about his dreams so many nights ago that had moved him to find the Elder. And he thought about meeting the Mage and returning to the Tapestry of Spirit.

And with these thoughts and hopes and desires, he extended his closed hand outward and then opened it, releasing the Heart Stone to fall to the soil of the World. He opened his eyes and looked down to where it lay.

It pointed East.

And in looking to the East, the boy's heart had spoken.

Throughout the afternoon, the boy's Destiny Thread led him to cross the same river on several more occasions as it gently turned back and forth, meandering toward the East. And with each crossing of the river, the same river that he had crossed with the dying Elder the night prior, the boy was mindful, as the Elder had instructed him to be during their first crossing of the river many days earlier.

With each step of each crossing, the boy was deliberate and patient, intent to experience the state of being in the water as he moved through it. And with each crossing, the boy's heart knew that he waded through that which was returning to Nature, the water from the mountain snow finding its way to the Sea, just as the boy was finding his way back to his Nature.

As the Sun approached the horizon in the West, the gentle curving of the river had ceased, and then only came directly from the East. And with his crossings of the river complete, the boy now journeyed alongside it, and noticed that as he journeyed beside it in the remainder of the day's light, the river became gradually smaller and narrower, now a small stream instead of the river that it earlier had been.

And the changing of the river to a stream beside him was odd, for along his journey that day, no smaller streams had joined it, and it was not natural for a flow of water to become smaller and narrower as one journeyed toward its source. It was not something that the boy could understand.

By nightfall, the boy lay next to the stream, his head resting upon his pack, and he looked up into the starry sky. He thought of what the Elder had said in the morning hours on the day of his death, how on the evening of what was now just the following day, the boy would somehow be in the presence of his Mother again. And it was with thoughts of her that the boy closed his eyes and fell asleep.

❧ 24 ❧

On the next morning, the boy woke with a sensation that was vaguely familiar, yet distant over the recent seasons of his life: a simple sensation of awareness.

There, lying on the ground, the boy heard the gleeful song of waking birds, saw the streaks of first light as they stretched from their slumber in the East, and felt the tickling breeze of the morning as it feathered over him. And with this simple sensation of awareness, the boy felt as if he hadn't departed from Nature while he slept, rather that he had joined with it, waking with the feeling that he and his Nature were again one, as they had been when he was a child.

After eating, he again wondered if East were still the course, but with less uncertainty than he had the previous morning, because on this morning, the boy's desire to meet the Mage and return to the Tapestry of Spirit were so present within him that he felt almost certain in his heart about continuing to the East. But, to be sure, he once again decided to summon the wisdom of the Heart Stone.

As he had done the previous morning, the boy closed his eyes, the Heart Stone held closely to his chest, while he thought deep inside himself of what he desired most, and extended his arm to drop the stone to the soil of the World.

And as had happened the prior morning, the boy opened his eyes and looked to the stone before him to again find that it pointed to the East. And with that, the boy thought not only of the wisdom of the stone, but of the wisdom of his own heart, for it was also East that the boy's heart believed his course to be. He began to understand what the Wholy Woman had said about the Heart Stone, that it would tell the boy what his own heart already knew.

For the entire day, the boy journeyed beside the stream as it flowed directly from the East, and as he had noticed during his travels beside it, the stream continued to get smaller and narrower, continuing to perplex the boy.

As the Sun began to set to the West, the boy sat by the stream and felt a deep connection to all things. It was as if all of the experiences of the journey had coalesced within him, as well as the events of his past, and as he sat and looked to everything around him, he could not help but see how woven together all things were, including the essence of the Elder that remained with the boy.

It had been several seasons since being distanced from it, but now the boy found himself returned to peace.

And in feeling such peace, the boy wondered if what he was feeling was the presence of his Mother, as the Elder had said would happen. He wondered if the things he had felt for the entirety of that day—the connection to things, the awareness, and the calm—were indeed his Mother's presence. He believed it to be so, for in his heart, sitting there by the river, he felt hope of what lie ahead, that it could hold whatever he desired it to hold, just as he had felt when a boy, in her presence, with each rising of the Sun.

And in that moment, as the boy thought of these things, a Colibri bird appeared and flew in to hover in front of him. And as the bird hovered before him, it tilted its head to look at the boy, and with a smile from the boy, the bird flew off and disappeared.

That evening, as the boy lay beside the stream, his last thought before falling to sleep was that he would meet the Mage on the following day.

During the night, the boy dreamt of his Mother. In the dream, with dawn approaching, she stood before him there by the stream where he had fallen asleep, her back to the East, and she was as she had been the last time he had seen her alive: happy.

As the first rays of the rising Sun lit the sky behind her, she was surrounded in a brilliant light which somehow was not painful or blinding to look upon. As she stood before him, she simply smiled at him, nothing more. No words were spoken. She held out her hands, and the boy gently took her hands into his, and he was home again, and a young boy again.

As the boy lay, dreaming his dream next to the stream that morning, light from the rising Sun in the East fell upon him, and although he woke from his dream, he could still feel his Mother's hands in his.

And upon awakening from the simple dream, the boy's mind echoed with words that she had spoken to him in the past, that one day, he would realize the beautiful gifts that he could offer to the World.

And it was then that he understood what he had not understood up to that moment. He understood how this was to happen.

That over the seasons since her passing, the boy had attempted to change himself so that he could exist within the World of men, believing that if he did so, he would conjure and offer the gifts to the World that she spoke of.

But what the boy realized in his awakening that morning was that in attempting to exist within the World of men, he had in fact closed off to the World the very gifts that he could offer.

And it was then clear to the boy that what his Mother saw within him, and had shared her wisdom of, was that indeed the boy did have beautiful gifts to offer, those that naturally resided within him, but they did not require anything of the boy but to be himself, for within his true self lie the most beautiful of gifts for the World, as do the gifts of all people.

And in being himself, the boy followed his Destiny Thread, and in following his Destiny Thread he would return to the Tapestry of Spirit, and he would once again be in accord with his Nature, as when a child.

And with this clarity of himself, the boy's belief in the direction of his course that day was strong, his heart having no doubt that he would again journey East, so much so that he found no need to summon the wisdom of the Heart Stone that morning.

❧ 25 ❧

Throughout the morning's journey, the boy reflected on his dream and the simple wisdom within it that would now be integral to his life. And as he continued to walk beside the stream, it continued to become smaller and narrower from where it came, still confounding the boy.

At mid-day, while sitting beside the stream for a meal, he noticed a single, beautiful white cloud adrift in the sky to the East. It was as billowy and bright a cloud as the boy had ever seen, and the fact that it was the sole cloud in the sky made it even more noticeable to him. And in seeing it, a memory returned to the boy, one from his first day of the journey when the cloud from the East approached as he was preparing to leave his home, the cloud that would rain down upon him gently and cleanse him. It seemed to the boy now that the gentle rain cloud at the beginning of his journey had a mate near its conclusion, one that was now in the sky to the East ahead of him, yet this cloud held no rain, nor did it need to.

In the early afternoon, with the boy walking beside the stream, the single cloud in the East that he had seen at midday had passed by overhead and caught the Sun as it made its way across the sky and toward the West. And when it did, all around the boy grew dim in the shadow of the cloud. He paused and looked behind him to see the cloud completely obscuring the Sun, yet there shone a single ray of light through the heart of the cloud, casting itself ahead of the boy and to the East.

The sight struck the boy, and he was in awe of what Nature had displayed before him. But to the boy's surprise, the cloud did not continue on, thereby closing its heart within that allowed the ray of Sun to pass through. Instead, as the boy waited for many moments, it appeared as if now the cloud and the Sun moved in harmony toward the West, all the while continuing to cast a single ray of light to the East, not far ahead of the boy.

Words came to the boy's mind that Nature would show him the way, and with that, the boy realized without thinking that where the light from the Sun touched the soil of the World ahead of him to the East, the Mage would be waiting.

The boy continued on, watchful for where the cloud and the Sun now directed him, and before long, he saw his destination.

Directly before him and up on a small hillside was a small, rocky outcropping, unlike its green surroundings. Not only did the narrow light from the Sun remain upon it, but the small stream of water that the boy still walked beside originated from it.

The boy continued toward it, climbing beside the small stream which was by then no wider than an arm's length as it rose up the hillside toward the outcropping. As the boy reached the opening, he found it to be the only thing illuminated in the surrounding shadow of the cloud.

Beyond the jagged, uneven rocks that surrounded the opening, there was a cove, recessed into the hillside, with the stream that the boy had journeyed beside for the past three days meandering back into its dimness.

And in looking into the darkened recesses of the cove, the boy's mind was back to his dream so many nights prior, the dream that prompted his meeting of the Elder. And how in the dream, after first being in the empty marketplace, he was next somewhere within the World, below its soil, for the meeting of the Mage.

The boy carefully stepped into the narrow cove, beside the stream that originated from somewhere within it, and paused for his eyes to adjust. After a moment, he began his way back into the recesses, and in that instant, another memory surfaced in the boy. He thought back to how much dread he had felt when entering the cold, dark Passageway of Shadows back in the belly of the snowy mountains. Yet now, as the boy stepped into the darkness of this cove, he felt warmth and hope and possibility.

And as the boy stepped deeper into the World, it struck him that it was actually becoming warmer, not colder, and the boy noticed that in the dimness, more and more vegetation grew on the walls, floor, and along the small stream that was shrinking to then just a fast trickle that he stepped beside.

A few steps more and the boy detected the faint sound of water dripping gently ahead of him. He made his way back toward the sound of the water, and with what light there was, he finally reached its origin.

The back of the cove widened into something of a circular shape, its entirety covered in a green moss. Around the back half of its circumference to the East, near the ceiling of the cove, protruded a row of end-to-end natural stones, forming something of a narrow, half-circular shelf above the boy's head. It was along this high shelf that partially encircled the depths of the cove, and from it, that water dripped, its origin unknown to the boy, to then fall into a small, shallow, half-circular pool in the floor of the cove. And with each drop of water that fell from the height of the cove and into the pool below, the surface of the pool shimmered in the dim lighting, making it as if alive.

From the front edge of the pool, the boy saw that a small trickle was born from the water that collected within it. It was this trickle that ran the length of the cove, out from its entrance, and down the sloping hillside to become the stream, and then the river, that the boy had journeyed beside and across along his journey.

The boy continued back toward the pool and the half-ring of dripping water, with each of his steps somehow bringing more and more water from along the shelf of stones above, and into the pool. And with each step, the back of the cove slowly brightened, for more and more light from the setting Sun outside of the cove and to the West was finding a clear pathway in.

With the boy a single step from the pool, he stopped. Now, the half-ring of dripping water had become a solid, semi-circular wall of water, falling steadily, filling the pool and feeding the growing trickle of water that left from its front edge. The light from the setting Sun, behind the boy and outside of the cove, now passed directly over his head and into the heart of the walls of water, illuminating the entire half-ring and the pool below it.

The scene was just as the boy had dreamt so many nights prior, before meeting the Elder and commencing the journey.

And there, standing before the half-ring of water that fell from the height of the cove, and looking to its center to the East, the boy saw a shape within it.

Slowly, the shape began to take a form, and the boy's heart quickened. The shape within the wall of water to the East began to resemble a man...a man in Mage's garb.

The boy was ready for his meeting of the Mage. He was ready to realize the outcome of his journey, not just the journey with the Elder, but the bigger journey that was only beginning for the seasons of his life that lie ahead. He was ready to realize and return to the Tapestry of Spirit.

And with one more step forward, the boy entered into the path of the light from the Sun, illuminating him from behind as he stood in front of the wall of water. The image of the Mage then came into full view and clarity.

It was a reflection of the boy himself.

And in that instant, all things became clear.

That he, and all people, are Mages. And as Mages, they possess the simple yet powerful ability of being able to see and perceive and believe in whatever they may choose to conjure within themselves, that the mystical vision of the heart is far deeper and truer than the vision of the eye, and that by summoning the vision of the heart, an individual life following a single Destiny Thread can be transformed into a life lived within the Tapestry of Spirit across the World. And that Spirit exists all around, in both the complex but especially the simple, and we need only summon our Mage's abilities to use the vision of our hearts to see it.

That the single strand that the Sage had said was at the heart of all Destiny Threads and therefore the Tapestry of Spirit, connecting them all, making all things possible, was indeed a simple thing: compassion. For compassion had been a part of the boy's entire journey, evident in the events along the way that had shown him so much of himself, and of how the World could be. That there is not a Spirit in the World that does not respond to compassion, and because of that, it is the single strand that is at the core of all Destiny Threads and therefore the Tapestry of Spirit.

And that with compassion, it was as the Wholy Woman had said, that we all are healers, for all people feel the presence of the Tapestry of Spirit when they offer and receive compassion, and with compassion and the healing that it enables, the suffering of the World can be healed, and the Tapestry of Spirit restored.

And while there exists a Fabric of People by virtue of shared and overlapping time during their existence in the World, their recognition of their connection to each other reveals the inherent and undeniable Tapestry of Spirit. That every Spirit upon the World, regardless of their age, tribe, or region of the World, shared of all other Spirits, were woven of the same, and could either inflict suffering upon each other, thereby unraveling the Tapestry, or help each other to heal, thereby restoring it.

The boy realized that his impact to the World was purely and simply of his own choosing, and that his legacy with the World around him could either be to add light or to add darkness, to either enhance the Tapestry or degrade it, and that he himself would reap what he offered to the World, be it good or bad. That as he offered to the World, so the World would offer to him.

And from these realizations, the boy again looked to the wall of water before him.

A moment prior, the boy saw a Mage in the wall of water come into focus, and then turn into the boy, and he witnessed that the Mage had turned into himself.

But now, the boy saw himself in the reflection and realized that he himself had turned into the Mage.

Whereas his vision of the eye saw a boy, his vision of the heart saw a Mage.

And with these things always to be recognized within him from that moment forward, the boy realized that to follow and live one's Destiny Thread, with honor for the strand of compassion at its core, and be one whose actions and words worked to restore the Tapestry of Spirit instead of unravel it, all that one need do is to heed their Heart Stone.

As the clarity of the realizations from the boy's journey filled him, tears came to his eyes, but not tears of sadness, rather of joy. He understood the Tapestry of Spirit and his inclusion within it, and as the Elder had told him at the beginning as they sipped tea back in the marketplace so many days journey from where he stood, the World to the boy would forever be different. And the boy now knew what the Elder meant, that the World to the boy would forever be a *better* place.

The boy emerged from the passageway on the side of the hill with a deep sense of himself. He stood there for a long while and looked along the water that gently moved beside him and down the side of the hill to form the stream and eventually the river. And in thinking of how the water grew to a stream and then to a river, all the while doing so seemingly unnaturally, growing in size the further from its origin it journeyed, the boy realized why it was so.

He realized that he was as the water was, and that in fact, all those following a Destiny Thread with compassion at its core and living within the Tapestry of Spirit, were as the water was. For the water originated from a single place, following its Natural path as it journeyed, enriching those around it as it meandered, its path taking it along many things. Such was living a Destiny Thread within the Tapestry of Spirit.

And as one's Destiny Thread meanders with time and distance, and with compassion at its core, its influence, its benefit, its effects will grow and grow, just as the water did as it turned from trickle to stream to river, to touch more and more Spirits as it went, healing the World.

The boy felt anew again, as if a child, although with much greater wisdom than a child, or, as the boy pondered, with the wisdom needed to remain the perfection that was a child. The day was darkening to an end, but each day beyond would be as light and as open and as new as they had been in his youth, for each would now hold a recognition of his Destiny Thread, the compassion at its core, and the Tapestry of Spirit that all are a part of.

His thoughts of what the Sun would bring from the East in the morning entered his mind. He pulled the Heart Stone from his pack and looked at it, its color now a deep ruby in the fading light of the day. He closed his eyes, held the stone tightly in his hand and near to his chest, then thought deeply about what direction his longing pointed him toward, where his Spirit sought to journey.

He asked himself in honesty if he felt compassion in his heart in what he sought, as with which, the Heart Stone would point his course, a course that his own heart already knew, as the Wholy Woman had said. And with these thoughts and feelings, he gently dropped the stone from his hand and opened his eyes.

On the ground before him, the Heart Stone again pointed East, and the boy smiled.

In the morning, he would continue the journey to the East in search of the girl he had dreamt, and then met, the one whose eyes he shared, the one who journeyed as he did.

www.ingramcontent.com/pod-product-compliance
Lightning Source LLC
Chambersburg PA
CBHW020108180626
46812CB00006B/2514